by BARRY N. MALZBERG

NOVELS

Screen
Oracle of the Thousand Hands
The Confessions of Westchester County

SCIENCE-FICTION NOVELS

The Falling Astronauts
Overlay
Revelations
Beyond Apollo
Herovit's World

as K. M. O'DONNELL

The Empty People
Final War and Other Fantasies
Universe Day
Dwellers of the Deep
Gather in the Hall of the Planets
In the Pocket and Other Science Fiction Stories

Herovit's
World

Herovit's World

BARRY N. MALZBERG

Random House–New York

Library of Congress Cataloging in Publication Data

Malzberg, Barry N
   Herovit's world.

   I. Title.
PZ4.M2615He [PS3563.A434]   813'.5'4   72-11447
ISBN 0-394-48141-0

For Lee Wright
and Robert P. Mills

The sphere darted to the surface with an awful rush and as Mack Miller regarded it he knew right away that he was dealing with something absolutely new in the experience of the Survey Team with this sphere. He was dealing, in fact, with something which was possibly so alien and bizarre that it could defy the knowledge of anyone on Earth!

Nevertheless, he thought, as he proudly stepped forward to greet the aliens, he would do the best he could. That was all that was ever asked of a Surveyman. That was usually enough.

Would it be enough now? Or was it too late?

Kirk Poland: *Survey Starlight*

Herovit's
World

There's A Long Way Between Declining
and Death.   *Isaac Bashevis Singer*

Herovit's World

1

At the second annual cocktail party of the New League
for Science-Fiction Professionals, Jonathan Herovit finds
himself accosted by two angry readers who also despise his
work. "You stink, Herovit. You've been doing this damned
crap for so long it molders, and you'd better get yourself
out of science fiction before we throw you out," the taller
and stronger of the readers says ... and, quite possibly
drunk, hurls more than half a glass of scotch and soda into
Herovit's thin, querulous face; then, realizing the apparent seriousness of the action, he apologizes suddenly and
backs away, his face now fallen to sadness, looking just like
Mack Miller's when the Team came across a seemingly
insoluble problem. "But then again ..." the boy says.
"Well, then again, I guess everybody has a right to *live.*"

The other reader, a girl similarly dressed, touches Herovit by her vague expression of concern. "You shouldn't
take this too seriously, Mr. Herovit," she says. "Bill's just

3

so involved with all of you writers and science fiction, but the fact is that you are losing your grip just a little, don't you think?" Then she leaves the room quickly, dragging the trembling Bill by the hand.

No one seems to have noticed this. All of the Science-Fiction Professionals are off in corners with editors or antagonists, promoting their careers, renewing old hatreds. Herovit takes a handkerchief from a rear pocket, shakes it open in spurts, and begins careful work on the stain which is already congealing rather thickly in places on his suit jacket. After a time of hopeless patting, however, he decides to leave it be.

It is a symbolic stain. He will wear it as a badge. Events in the room continue. Perhaps all of this occurred only in his mind or was otherwise hallucinative. This is what comes of having been a science-fiction writer for twenty years: it is difficult to take oneself altogether in earnest.

It is all typical of the kind of trouble he has been having recently and for quite a while back. He finishes his drink, wondering exactly how in hell readers were able to get into this party anyway. It was described in all of the mailings as a meeting for only the most serious editors and writers in the field, those who were central to science fiction and who, each in his own way, were completely dedicated to its advancement.

2

That night, after the party, Herovit has a dream about the boy who threw scotch in his face, and wakes from it in a series of terrified gasps, realizing that it is the first real critical feedback he has received in many years—or at least since two of his novels were reviewed favorably in the monthly science-fiction department of a West Coast newspaper (". . . also sure to be on your favorite s-f buff's Christmas list would be these two latest by the ubiquitous Kirk Poland . . ."). He reaches for his wife beside him, resolved to tell her what has happened to him and thus inaugurate a serious discussion on this life which he has shaped, but he realizes at the last moment as his fingers graze the girl beside him that he has been engaging in casual adultery for many years and that the young fan, now sleeping peacefully in his hotel bed, could react only with surprise or rage if she awoke to find Jonathan Herovit groaning out confessions of inadequacy into the small of her back. Word would quickly get around certain circles that he was losing his grip.

Herovit rears in the bed and turns the other way. He resolves that over the weeks to come he will carefully consider his place in the field, and if things continue to look as bad as they do at this moment, he will most definitely begin to think about considering the possibility of perhaps getting temporarily out of the game. He will. He will.

He sleeps.

3

More and more as he edges forty—now thirty-seven, nothing quite as it used to be biologically and otherwise— Herovit feels like a main character in one of his old serials for *Tremendous Stories.* Events press upon him; utterly alien and bizarre forces impinge. His grip, like Mack Miller's, is loosening through too many bad episodes. The very fabric of his existence is rent; still, what else is there to do? His public depends upon him. He must press on in order to resolve matters and bring a good report to Headquarters.

The trouble is—he is beginning to admit that he has trouble—that the characters in his serials always had machinery. In the hold, in some abscess of the ship or available by plans to one of the engineers, was a device which could be used to disperse the aliens once they got it going; failing all else, the alien forces menacing old Mack (he wishes that he could meet old Mack so that he, Jonathan Herovit, could kill him) would turn out to have had benign motives from the start. It was simple: put it together at 15,000 words and sell it to Steele; string it up to 60,000 and go for the book rights. Or both. Why not? Usually both. You could always get book rights on something Steele bought if you were willing to sink low enough.

But Mack Miller's case—always remember this—is not his own. Herovit can hardly use machinery to escape the circumstances surrounding, and whatever the nature of those mysterious forces, they are hardly benign. (At odd moments he can feel them clambering inside; benignity is not their custom.) Nevertheless, like Mack Miller, he must press on, if for different reasons.

Press on. He is one of the ten to fifteen most prolific science-fiction writers in the country, with an audience of somewhere between seventy to eighty thousand for the paperbacks—to say nothing of the magazines. How many truly serious writers had that much of an audience? Did seventy thousand read Stanley Elkin? Evan Connell? There they are, stuck in hardcover—where ten thousand was a remarkable sale and paperback came late, if ever— while Herovit is a mass-market writer. People read him on buses and in public rest rooms. It could hardly be the fault of his career that all of this was happening to him; rather, he must look elsewhere, into the root causes. Still, it was hard to do this kind of job; most of his characters were not at all introspective. Introspection would only hold back the plot.

In his more surreal moments, Herovit feels that the West Side of the city itself has become an alien planet, populated by archetypes or artifacts speaking languages

he does not know with gestures which can only terrify . . .
but he has a wife and now, damn it, a child; he is committed to Manhattan since it is central to his life, to say nothing of his work, and he pushes off these moments as
neurasthenia. Once he had looked it up in a medical dic-
tionary. It was a great word. It gave dignity to his situation.

4

Herovit pushes on past page forty of his new Mack
Miller Survey Team novel, which Branham Books hopes to
publish under his pseudonym of Kirk Poland. Originally,
he had wanted to write science fiction exclusively under
his own name, but John Steele, the venerable editor of
Tremendous Stories when Herovit broke in, had advised
him that *Jonathan Herovit* did not have the right sound
for the image of the magazine being developed, and it
would be best to use a pseudonym with which the engineers and disturbed adolescents who read *Tremendous*
could fully identify.

"You see, son, Jonathan Herovit sounds too urban, uh,
too European and cosmopolitan for this book," Steele had
said, winking madly and lifting his enormous arms toward
the ceiling as he expanded his large chest with cigarette
smoke. "It has a very New-Yorkish type of ring, if you
follow what I'm trying to say here, and our magazine goes
nationwide. We even do nicely in the South, and then the

Army picks up thousands of copies for overseas distribution through regular channels."

Herovit—no fool he—guessed that he had gotten the implication. "Sure," he said, "I guess that we could shorten it, then, to something Germanic like *John Herr* once I start selling. Or even—"

"Now what you want, son," Steele said, "is something which is all-American." He had a very bad habit, Steele did, of continuing a line of discussion no matter what the response, but this, Herovit had decided, was one of the elements of the man's greatness. Why *should* a John Steele listen when his circulation was in the high sixties and everyone else's in the low forties or worse? Sure he was being pushed a little by the newer magazines like *Thrilling* or *Thoughtful,* but he was still the grand old man of the field, always would be. "Maybe just a little trace of the peculiar on the edges, something exotic, you know, but never threatening for the guys. If you can't think up a good one on your own I'll decide for you like I've done for a lot of the others, but first you'll have to sell me a yarn, of course. That always comes first, doesn't it? I'm a little overstocked now but you're certainly welcome to try. Anyone's welcome to *try,* got to keep on pushing for the new blood," Steele had said and then sent Herovit—at that time twenty-two and single—on his way from the gigantic chain of pulp-magazine offices in which Steele's cubicle had been in an insignificant place, wedged between the mailroom and a messenger's comfort station.

Herovit had at the time been extremely anxious to break into science fiction, so he had listened to everything Steele had to say. This was not only a matter of achieve-

ment: he had just then been fired from a probationary
position with the New York City Department of Welfare,
and at this period in his life saw absolutely no way of
generating the fast income he needed unless he could
work into the pulp market, which no one knew was then
on the verge of complete collapse.

Thus he had settled—too much pride to let Steele pick
his name—on *Kirk Poland* both because some kind of
trouble in the damned Gomulka government was making
the newspapers at that time, and his landlord, a creditor
at that time, had been named Joe Poland. Under that
name—Kirk, not Joe this was—he had sold Steele his first
novelette only a month after their conference. Kirk was a
good first name. Nothing insoluble could ever happen to
a man named Kirk once he put his mind to things.

Subsequently, Herovit had sold five hundred and three
additional magazine pieces as well as ninety-two science-
fiction novels, all of them by Kirk, whom he had visualized
from the start (perhaps in a dream, although origins had
never been his strong point) as a tall, thin guy, fairly wiry,
with devastating hands and huge sunken eyes. A guy who
never had trouble coming, be it fast or slow. Sex stuff, on
the other hand, Kirk had never been able to write; it gave
him (or at least it gave Herovit) cold sweats and a livid
feeling of embarrassment—a sensation that his mother-in-
law, for instance, was inspecting copy over his shoulder as
it came from the typewriter. Now that the sex market is
gone, and it is entirely too late to crawl from under the
pseudonym to find another identity, however, Herovit regrets following Steele's suggestions so unquestioningly.
On his own, he might have been a fine writer.

But then again (and he reminds himself of this all the time), there are many thousands, if not millions, of people who have tried and failed to make full-time careers as writers, so he certainly has a lot to be thankful for, even if he only made eleven thousand, four hundred dollars last year, and only a very few sophisticated fans and readers in the field know that it is he, Jonathan Herovit, who originated Mack Miller's Survey Team. Not Kirk Poland. In seventeen years of professional writing, Kirk has received exactly twelve fan letters and one sexual proposal from a woman who said that she was forty-one years old but devoted to machinery and, thanks to Process Training administered in the middle 1950's, still quite ready to go.

"Lothar, go down below and examine the table of elements. Check it out thoroughly to f ind if tanamite can be found on it. Do this right away, crewman," the Captain said determinedly in his quiet voice, Herovit now writes and then comes again to a dead halt in this accursed ninety-third novel. He must establish the physical-science basis for the plot at this point. The thing to do—he has been this way so many times before; why then is it bothering him so?—is type a long scene between the Captain and his first mate, Lothar, both of them highly unsympathetic aliens, explaining the mysterious substance that one hundred and fifty-nine pages later will signal their doom . . . but Herovit, looking at the twenty-first page in the typewriter, realizes that he cannot do it. Not yet again. Is there such a thing as tanamite or is it a fool's construct? Lothar wondered idly as he then scurried off in loyal slave's fashion to do his captain-master's bidding. He is not up to this really, not at all. He cannot face one more line of exposition, nor is there any way in which he can take either of these characters seriously, Lothar and the Captain being individuals who under various names have already been included in at least seventy-three full-length, never-before-published adventures. Someday he would take his revenge upon the Captain and it would be terrible, restoring the balance between them, but it could not be on this expedition, Lothar feared, listening to the hum of those giant engines as tirelessly they brought them ever closer to their destination and the inevitable conflicts which awaited. He simply cannot do this kind of thing any more.

The trouble is (and he might as well face it; he will not be a self-deceiving man) that he is falling apart. Through the clear and dark portholes, shaped like abcissa, he could see the constellations of a different galaxy, sense a thousand new suns and the adventures which would follow. The thought of them filled him with humility and awe, low-rated as he was. The psychic strain of production, the insularity of the field of science fiction, and the difficulties in his own personal life have closed around him within recent months; now Herovit is not so sure that he can take himself, let alone his work, seriously. It was something

to think about, the look of those stars.
Few had gazed upom them, fewer still
would return to the familiar galaxies to
bear the tale. The novel which he is supposed to be
writing is number twenty-nine in the Survey Team Con-
queror Series. For this, his agent has negotiated a standard
advance of two thousand dollars as against four and six
percent of paperback royalties, payable one thousand
upon signature and another thousand on delivery. He
needs that second thousand desperately and is already
forty-five days late (compulsively he counts everything) on
the delivery, but he finds that the very thought of plowing
on with this novel, to say nothing of actually finishing it,
makes him quite ill. Twenty-one pages completed (of
course he never rewrites) and a month and a half late. This
is pitiful, no doubt about it.

This is pitiful. Truly pitiful, Lothar
finds himself thinking and thinking then
for the twenty-ninth time that if only
Colonial Survey had not been so author-
itarian he would have had his last slave-
voyage several moons ago. He hopes that
this thinking is not an omen of worse
things to come but suspects that as always his mood is a good barometer of what
will follow.

Heat sneezes in the pipes of Herovit's office. He hears
his wife of a decade again cursing their six-month-old
daughter. Herovit can make out some of the words. Lothar thought that he could make out some

of the words the Captain was saying in re-
lation to his slave-status, and he tried
to block all of them out of his mind. He
did not want to hear them.

He decides to leave the Captain, not to say Lothar, to
their own devices for a time. The bottle of scotch is on his
desk. He drinks.

5

That night he tries again rather reluctantly but persis-
tently to get things started again in the sex department
with his wife, but Janice turns from him deftly, talking,
inexhaustibly talking, as he tries to fondle her breasts and
finally, in disgust, quits.

"I won't have any of that," she says in a high voice,
protecting herself, "and who do you think you are anyway,
Jonathan? I'm at the end of my patience, you know. You
can't ignore me during the day and treat me like some
kind of housekeeper—some kind of *housekeeper,* that was
the word I wanted to use, and you'd better not miss it—
and then expect me to be passionate on your demand, can
you? Is this normal thinking? Do you really think that
you're being quite rational? You have some sensitivity left
in you, I hope, so you must think that I'm really quite
stupid or that I've got such lust for you that I can't resist,

but that isn't a good way of looking at it. I gave up everything for you and all that you can do is think that I'm an object for your desires. I'm a slave without any pay, that's all I am!"

Since the pregnancy and subsequent birth of their daughter Natalie, which forced Janice's resignation from the product division of a second-rate public relations agency, she has been quite nervous and hard-edged, and most of her conversation sounds like this. Janice was never (Herovit, in his senescence, now admits *everything*) what one might call an accessible or highly sympathetic figure, but now, in her discovered role as the thirty-five-year-old mother of an ill-tempered, bottle-fed, cereal-spitting infant, she seems to have collapsed into a set of attitudes which were probably always waiting to absorb her. Also, she hates science fiction. This is strange, considering that Herovit met her at a convention fifteen years ago when she was chairlady of the Bronx Honor John Steele Society and Steele himself was the guest of honor.

"You think about me only when you want something and you never know I'm alive any other time," she says, rotating and shoving her buttocks at Herovit . . . but not at all invitingly. Mack Miller would never have to take this shit. Of course Mack Miller, at least on the record, had never been laid yet, but if he *had* been laid you could be sure that he would be in the dominant position.

"I'm sorry," he says mildly. He is not Mack Miller. Increasingly these days he seems to be apologizing and, what is worse, meaning it. Herovit's regrets and sense of culpability are real: he knows that he, and no one else, has made his life. "I only thought that I might, uh, hold you, you know, like that. Nothing else. I know that you're tired, what you're going through, but of course, as you should know, I've kind of got problems myself and—"

"You don't know anything. You can't know anything if you think that I care for your problems with that crap. Do you know what I'm going through? Do you know what the bitch is doing to me?" Janice refuses to call the baby by her name; it is always *the bitch, the kid, the thing,* or at best, *the infant*—thus, Herovit supposes, depersonalizing the situation somewhat and thus protecting her emotions. He does not know an awful lot of psychology—that not being the strong point of his writings, which focus on the hard sciences—but he can make an assumption or two, or so he guesses.

"No," he says, not wanting the discussion which is now coming but knowing with ten years' cunning that this discussion may be his only pathway into her and that if he has any interest in his wife at all he must *discuss* his way into sex. Hear her complaints one by one as a means of penance in advance. "Tell me what she's doing to you. Did she do anything bad to you today, for instance?"

"What do you care anyway? What difference does it make? I'm a fool to think that you're even interested in any of this."

"But I am interested. I really am. She's *our* daughter, the two of us together, right? It can't be one but both." These are certain ritual matters to attend to before there is even the possibility of sex. Herovit sighs and wishes, not for the first time, that he were a more industrious adulterer. As it is, he is little more than a dilettante, a hobbyist, picking up scraps where he may, but this is not the correct approach for the serious-minded. Still, even at the level of science fiction, adultery can become very expensive, so he may have less complaints than he thought.

"You. All day you're locked up like a rat in that office of yours, typing up your crap and getting drunk. Mostly getting drunk, you're not even that *busy* any more. I can't hear the typewriter most of the time; you think I don't know what's going on in there? I'm aware of everything. But what do you know of my life? Can you understand what this thing is costing me every day now?"

"Oh yes," Herovit says. "Oh yes, I think I do. I do know what it's costing you. It isn't easy, not easy for me either," looking through the ceiling, past the screen of smoke from the cigarette he has been working on, thinking—thinking somewhere there must be a glade, somewhere there must be flowers, somewhere there must be animals bleating contentedly throughout the night and ships whisking over the water. Somewhere at this very moment such a place exists, and these things are happening there or not at all, and I must get what comfort I can from the knowledge that while they are there they count for something . . . someone somewhere is getting laid and it must be good.

Three stories beneath, a fire engine, sirens like imploded rockets, staggers past, and the odors of the city sweep like moths to nibble over him. What did he do to deserve this? All that he wanted was to make an easy buck. Simple Jonathan Herovit to come to such an end as this as he listens to his wife, listens to his wife, listens to his wife—

Talking.

6

In the morning his agent calls to say that the publisher is now beginning to press hard for delivery of the overdue Survey Team novel and that he (the agent that is, to say) also finds himself upset about the way things are going with Herovit. What has happened to his career? Where is the old sense of discipline? What does Herovit think: That just because he has sold ninety-two novels the world now owes him a living? Mack Miller would not have to take this shit; he would scream back at this old bastard over the phone and tell him a few things, but Herovit, owing six hundred dollars, merely listens. The world does not owe him a living. Perhaps he should quit novel-writing if this is all the responsibility that he can show in his late thirties. Get himself some kind of a job instead. Unless he is unemployable, which is most likely the case by now.

Herovit's agent is named Morton Mackenzie. Morton is fifty and represents more than half of the full-time science-fiction writers in the country, but considers himself more famous as a result of a short article about himself in a newsmagazine four years ago. This article included Mackenzie's photograph and noted that he had the largest collection of sixteen-millimeter science-fiction horror films in the world. There are intense rumors—have been for a long time—that Mackenzie, who is also an alcoholic, has never read a word of science fiction in his life and in fact hates it, but the field is full of gossip like this. Many people who write science fiction do not like the form, and why the hell should they? Still and all, Mackenzie is a grand old fellow. He has been at the center of the field, representing his writers in good times and evil, since his fifteenth birthday in 1937 or so, and Herovit at this time does not have the heart to further upset this important figure, who is in an excellent legal position to drop him as a client and sue for recovery of monies owed.

"I mean," Mackenzie says in a high bleat, causing the receiver to shake reciprocally in Herovit's damp palm two full miles uptown, "I mean this, I mean to say that I can't put up with this pressure any more. You're getting yourself quite a reputation for backing out on contracts, Jonathan, and if it ever comes right down to the wire I'll have to let you go. Business is business. There's a whole client list I've got to protect, not to mention my integrity and reputation for honesty in the field, and I can't have one client fucking me over like this. No one fucks me over! Although in the personal sense I'll always remain fond of you, remembering the man you were."

"I never backed out on a contract in my life," Herovit lies. "Excuse me," he then murmurs and pauses to light his fifteenth cigarette of the morning from the candle he has set burning to the left of his typewriter and the thirty-third completed page of *Survey Sirius.* Halfway down on the thirty-fourth. Eight thousand words in the can; perhaps he can get away with forty-two thousand if he uses wide margins and lots of dialogue, filling out the pages so cleverly that a stupid editor might take this for a full-length book. "I've been late five or six times. Okay, I'll grant that I take my time on the work, but it's always been for a good reason like having other commitments or wanting to do a careful job for its own sake. You have no right to say that and it isn't fair. It just isn't fair to me, Mack; have a sense of justice."

He realizes for the first time—how could he have missed this?—that the protagonist of the Survey books and his agent have the same nickname. Shouldn't he have noted this years ago? But then it would have to be some kind of pure coincidence; Herovit prides himself on the way in which he manages to keep his personal problems and his copy far apart. Only amateurs carry things over; professionals suppress personality conflicts mercilessly. And anyway, lots of characters and writers in science fiction had been named *Mack;* if he picked it up from the outside, it could as easily have been from there. Pure coincidence. He should not worry about this any more. Forget he ever brought it up.

"Always these goddamned rationalizations," Mackenzie screams. "Nothing's fair! Nothing's ever right for you! But what really isn't fair is having Branham Books jumping down old Mack's throat and accusing him of handling an unreliable client who sold them a novel in bad faith. I mean, I don't want to upset you or anything like that, Jonathan, but they're saying that if you don't get this book in now by the end of the week, they're going to void the contract and demand the advance back. This is an important market and I'm not going to lose them on your account."

Quite against his will, Herovit finds himself nodding. He knows what Mackenzie means here and the wonderful old fellow does have a point. Branham Books is not truly a publisher of science fiction but a large house primarily interested in reprints of best sellers and sex manuals for the intellectual. Only a few months ago, Branham contracted for a very few science-fiction novels to "investigate this exciting new market," one of the people aiding in the investigation being the deft Kirk Poland, whose agent had offered them the latest in the famous Survey Series. Now, if the editor at Branham had been one of the five or six familiar figures in the paperback field, Herovit would have been able to deal with him on his own: wheedle the man into a little more time, say, or play up the matter of personalities, make him feel guilty or try blackmail ... but the very gender, let alone personality, of this editor is unknown. He signs himself/herself *H. Smythe.* It would be impossible to even attempt an approach toward H. Smythe if there wasn't even a sex angle from which to approach it. ("H?" he imagines himself saying. "H, can we discuss this on a personal level of appeal, H?" No, this would not work at all.)

At the time of the sale Herovit had been very pleased, presuming that a house as large as Branham might go on for years before they noticed that a contract novel was undelivered, but this had been a mistake. Obviously they were so big and important because they pursued deliveries, even two-thousand-dollar deliveries, with vengeful passion. He will have to realign his thinking about this in the future.

"Oh, all right," he says, meanwhile. "Now the book happens to be coming along fine. In fact, right this minute I'm carefully finishing up the final draft, and it ought to be in your hands by Thursday. The beginning of next week, anyway, by the very latest. They aren't going to get us in trouble—a big house like that, an editor no one's ever heard of—for a matter of just a few days. This isn't any amateur they're threatening, you know, it's Kirk Poland." He tries to pace his voice, modulate, italicize, be as soothing and confident as possible, knowing better than almost anyone the wonderful old fellow's tendency to disintegrate under stress and to begin mumbling about the terms of his will, under which the Library of Congress itself is scheduled to receive his film collection and forty-three-year (so far) diary.

"Don't give me that crap!" Mackenzie is shouting. "You're not finishing up any second draft, you're not doing any polishing. You haven't done a second draft in your whole life! You're probably stuck on page thirty of some piece of crap, with a bottle on your desk and a dirty sheet in the typewriter. You know something, Jonathan, you've got yourself a little bit of a serious drinking problem on your hands. I've been meaning to point this out to you for months, and finally I don't want to hold it back. I've had a little trouble with booze myself in my time ... well, maybe more than a little trouble, but anyway it just makes me sensitive to your trouble. You'd better watch that stuff or it could be the end of a fine career—or at least a career. Now Jack Craggings didn't think that anything would hap-

pen to *him* either, but, well now, you just think of Jack
Craggings, a brilliant talent—"

"No, I won't," Herovit says loudly. "I won't think of
Craggings." He does not want to hear again (Mack always
brings this one out when he feels confidential and is a little
drunk himself) about poor Jack Craggings, who after a
single brilliant Tracer Tour novella which appeared in the
third issue of *Thrilling* and became the basis for a novel,
a movie, a television series and a Los Angeles production
of a full-length play, disintegrated due to overindulgence
on the fifteen thousand dollars he had netted from all of
this. Herovit himself had known Craggings vaguely and
doubted if the trouble was drink. Rather, it seemed to be
a wife problem or, more specifically, a third-wife problem
that had finished him off.

"Everything's under control, Mack," he says reassur-
ingly, knowing now that if his luck runs well he will be able
to harmonize with Mackenzie's solicitude and drive
straight through to the end of this conversation without a
reply. "Believe me, I know what sauce has done to a lot
of the guys; anyway, you're too smart for me. As a matter
of fact, I'm on page thirty-four, not thirty, but I'm just
starting to really hit, and I'm going to settle down now for
real and get this book out. A hundred pages a day, just like
the good old days; ten pages an hour right out of the
typewriter, really pouring out. Sixteen hours' work; I'll
stay right here and finish it up by three in the morning.
You'll love it and so will Branham Books," Herovit says and
very quickly hangs up on his agent.

His hands, in fact, begin to flutter only after the phone

is safely back on its hook. He yanks the phone jack out of
the wall, uncontrollable hands or whatever, determined to
avoid the fast ring back that is one of Mackenzie's special-
ties when he is in a certain mood ... and then confronts
the typewriter. Sighs deeply, a sigh which turns slowly
into a nauseated growl as he expels air, looking at what he
has done, at what he has made of his life.

Well. Nothing to do but go on with it. No one is going
to get him out of this. The capsule spun wildly
and uncontrollably in its tight orbit,
and for a moment, Mack felt disorien-
tated. True disorientation sped through
him and made him feel very weak. Then,
with a shudder, he willed himself to discipline and grounded himself to the
apogee.

Outside of the porthole he could see the
rising hues of Meldeberan VI. It was a
tough planet, Meldeberan was. A brutal
planet, one which had sent the best of the
regulars to destruction necessitating
that Survey be called in, as always, to
bail headquarters out. So that meant it
was a planet which a Survey man could
overcome ... if he only had the strength,
the will, the fire.

One of these days, Mack thought, if his
luck ran out, they were going to catch up
with him. And what would happen then?

End of chapter.

He lights yet another cigarette, takes a bubbling sip from the full tumbler of scotch that he—all good intentions—had brought into the office at eight, determined to make the most of the morning. When this is done he will have to go to the bottle itself and it is going very fast. In the good old days, of course, scotch seemed to act merely as a conductor, a set of filaments through which the writing could charge; now it seems, rather, to be loosening connections . . . but he needs it more than ever. No shame in it.

New chapter.

The powerful, loping stride of the Meldeberanin brought the beast ever closer to the small, dim ship on the edge of the plains. As it ate up the ground with surges of pure physical energy, flashes of power volting from its brutal and strangely shaped head. The Meldeberanin was five kilometers away or maybe a little less than that, closing the ground quickly, crackling ferociously when Mack took the laser out of its silicone case and zeroed in on the alien.

"might as well," Mack muttered to himself, thinking of what he had to do. A Surveyman, unlike the regulars, always prepared himself for the worst: killing was a necessary part of the job and he had no guilt. No sense in taking chances on a strange planet with its record of brutal slaughter, and if he were not willing to kill the aliens on sight he had no business making himself a Surveyman. The fools and clerks in headquarters, organized scientists most of them, would try to cloud over the issue with their ? liberal euphemistics, whining and shouting at the corpse of any alien (when the corpses of a thousand Earthers would be judged only an "unfortunate accident"). But Mack knew danger when he saw it. He was not an Establishment member, had no truck with sociology, and could recognize danger when he saw it.

Also he could recognize malevolence. Now through the amplificators of the ship he could hear the hoofs and greenish spurs of the Meldeberanin hitting the ground as it drew closer, and he shouted into his own amplificator the galactic signal to halt, which should be known to even the most backward of races since it had originated on earth.

The Alien did not halt, as Miller knew it would not, and therefore he shot it to death.

It occurs to Herovit that he had wanted to be a literary-type writer. Why not? He'd had important things to say, and the few Foley and O. Henry collections that he had looked at in his early twenties were obviously full of crap.

Anyone could do better than this stuff if he had the right connections. But the science-fiction market at that time had seemed so accessible, the magazines so easy to hit at the time he broke in (there were fifty of those magazines and anything typed cleanly in English with the word "space" in it somewhere could get placed, if only at a quarter of a cent a word on publication), that he had felt it was foolish to pass up the easy money on that account alone. He'd had it all figured out: what he was going to do was write science fiction for a couple of years, just to build up a good reputation in this simple field and some kind of financial backlog (if he could make, say, even seven thousand dollars a year he could save like crazy, living as he did in a furnished room), and then he would head out to the serious hardcover markets with a long novel of Army life that he had all blocked out in his head. Just had to put it down. The novel was so completely available to him that even now he could write it tomorrow. But who would give an advance?

So what he would do would be to raise a little margin on which to get to work. Even the individual scenes and characters were already cold. But the Meldeberanin did not stop, although the shot that it had taken was surely fatal. In fact it increased its speed, moving with frightful force over the darkening plains. Its features were cast in those of complete evil, and even though Mack was a Surveyman he felt the first tingling of what might have been fear.

Getting it down on paper would be nothing, but it would have been stupid to have passed up, just when he was getting started, a nice and enjoyable dollar. Had he at last met a challenge beyond him, a challenge which he could not overcome? Mack did not know.

7

Herovit looks at his daughter sleeping in the crib which had been the only baby furnishing that Janice and he had bought before the birth. (Oh, well; if they didn't prepare for it, it might not, despite all the visible indications, happen. That was the way they were thinking. Surely no harm in it; there was a little superstition in even the best of people.) The child is as alien as anything he has ever conceived, as mysterious as the surfaces of the sun ... but in the slow curl of palms and toes, in the twitching, absent smile which Natalie gives a dream, Herovit sees himself, and something churns. He feels a connection to the child, but this he does not even want to consider at the moment. He has a novel to do.

He leaves the baby's room quickly and quickly passes his wife without a look. Exhausted, she is sitting in the kitchen watching television—a quiz show he guesses—smiling as if in coma. Her body heaves. Herovit strides alertly downstairs into the West Eighties in determined search of an early-evening edition. It is noon, and certainly he deserves some kind of a break after all of the good work he has done this morning.

8

He receives a phone call from the girl with whom he slept in the hotel the evening of the League for Science-Fiction Professionals' cocktail party. She feels slightly embarrassed about calling him at home, knowing how busy a professional writer must be (probably turning out another one of those novels right this minute), but would like to know nevertheless if he would attend a meeting of the developing Staten Island Wonder Association, of which she is still the corresponding secretary and second chairman.

"Now you don't have to come if you don't want to," she says rather bitterly. "They only put me up to this job because they thought you might say yes if I asked, but if you don't want to come, it really doesn't mean a thing to me either. I don't care about any of that fan stuff, it's still for the kids. Why, I haven't even been active for over two years and I'm much older than the rest of them—too old for those meetings—but if I can do them a favor, well then, why not?" Her voice is hurt; Herovit feels that he has come into the middle of something quite complicated.

"Most of these people have no life outside of talking about science fiction, which is a rather sad thing when you think about it, but still, someone has to buy the stuff and read it, isn't that right? They put up the money."

Herovit recalls listening to this as he has not recalled for several days what it was like to be with her. (Sex departed is best forgotten; why get yourself all upset, although now and then you could come up with an image that you could jack off to.) She'd had resilient breasts and had not, even in the last throes of sex, made a sound. Maybe being a *Wonder* Reader conditioned you against ordinary novelties. Also, she does not seem to have read a word of his, not ever, which on that basis alone means that he owes her some affection and a sense of obligation. People who have never read him have done Herovit, he supposes, a rather large favor.

Fundamental detachment, however, must remain. It is the only quality which has made his adulteries possible through the years, not that there have been many of them and not, as he thinks back upon them randomly, that they have been very good at all. Most of the girls have been querulous and demanding. "You must understand, Gloria," he says—her name is coming back to him along with, oh God, just about everything else—"that I'm a happily married man. Well, fairly happily. Anyway, I can't really be called at home like this too frequently; it could lead to problems, you see, and furthermore—"

"Oh, that's all right. I know all about that part of the deal, and anyway I'm involved with someone who's just sort of into town. I know how these things work and believe me," she adds with a mysterious giggle, "I wouldn't want to get that whole thing started up again, if you follow what I'm saying. Once was enough in the relational context we established, two would press it out of context." Yes, most of his adulteries talk this way. "Look, if you don't want to make a meeting on Staten, that's okay too. I explained already that this thing wasn't even my idea. They just sort of asked me to call."

One of the problems with these people under twenty-five, Herovit has noticed, is their incessant *vagueness*. It seems to him that when he was younger (once he must have been younger, although this is a chronological statement only) he struggled to find a certain precision in his speech and thinking, aided very much by John Steele, who told all his writers to think *clearly*. Yet not only do these people seem perfectly content with their rhetoric, they appear to understand one another while he has trouble. "Sort of," the girl says again, and there is a hanging pause during which Herovit is able to contemplate more of his adulteries; they all jumble together, but an overriding impression of dullness remains. "Well," she says finally, "of course if that's all that I really meant to you—"

"Oh no," he says. He senses her retreat and with it the possibility of blackmail. Even the receiver now seems to be withdrawing subtly from his left ear, quite unlike its conduct with Mackenzie, when it seems to grow tendrils and go poking for latent cysts. "Don't be embarrassed about anything. It's perfectly all right." He may meet this Gloria at another party or convention someday, science fiction being such a confined world, and if that is the case, why not? He has probably been seeing but not noticing her at conventions for years before he ever took her to bed. It is always pleasant to maintain a sense of opportunity, strands of possibility to dangle from his progressively delimited life. "I don't mind making an exception in this one instance. It's just a general—well, you know—kind of *policy—*"

"I don't care about policies. What do policies mean to me? I don't even understand what you're talking about. A group of them were just suggesting that I should call. They said, 'Gloria, why don't you phone the guy and try him,' so I said, 'Okay, he seems like a pretty nice guy.' The actual truth is that I haven't been an active member for a really long time. This corresponding secretary job is just kind of an honorary one because of what I mean to the group, but I don't have to do a thing. Well, anyway—"

Ah, God, he cannot stand this any more. He really cannot. It is one thing to have hovered over this girl in the blissful hotel night, her body protecting him in its density from all of those unfriendly elements outside prone to tossing scotch in his face or something similar . . . it is quite another to deal with this girl in the more practical sense of conversation.

He has always made these kinds of misjudgments. The original and most serious error had been with Janice: he had actually believed that there would be some carry-over from the fucking to their relationship. What a mistake that had been! He must try to guard against this kind of thing in the future, although there is very little likelihood, at thirty-seven, that Herovit can truly change his life although he would like to try. "I'll come," he says meanwhile, leaving life-changing out of it. "I promise. I'll come.

With a set speech or something for your group. But I won't take any questions, you understand—I want to make that clear in advance. I have a kind of general approach to these meetings which I've developed over the years, and I pretty much have to stick to it. For everyone's good. You'll see what I mean when I do it."

"That's no problem."

"And it definitely couldn't be for a couple of weeks . . . Well, not until the end of next week, anyway; it would have to wait until then. What I'm doing, you see, is wrapping up this big novel for a major publisher and—"

"Oh, that's all right," Gloria says, coming in so quickly after "big novel" that he inhales in surprise, takes a sickening amount of scotch directly into his lungs and coughs. "That doesn't bother them or me at all. I'm not really talking about anything so soon. They're just trying to set things up for the winter after next on this long-range schedule being drawn up."

"Long-range? Schedule?"

"Actually, they have quite a few people lined up already for this kind of thing, and they're just trying to get possible replacements if any one of them should fall through, you dig? Anyway, we know how you stand now and that's the important thing. Thanks for taking an interest in us," Gloria says in businesslike, detached tones and cuts off the conversation. Maybe she did not hang up so abruptly. Maybe just at that moment, by coincidence, the connection failed. Sure. That is the only reasonable explanation.

Herovit is left breathing into the mouthpiece on the solitary. In the even curl of his breath, he perceives the rhythms and little interruptions of sex, and this is so stunning a perception that he resolves to make peace at any cost with Janice this afternoon so at the very least he will have something to which to look forward tonight. Why not? She is not the best lay going—never was even in her prime—but she is something at least, and he can hardly plow ahead on this miserable novel without the thought of something to even out the edges of the day.

Child or no child. The child has nothing to do with this situation. He is still entitled to some satisfaction. He has rights under the marital contract. Procreation is not the sole basis of sexuality, now is it? Regardless of your religion.

9

But Janice will not listen. She will not listen even when he tries to appeal to her better nature and sense of fairness. He goes to sleep, petulantly and tumescently alone, while she stays in the kitchen and watches television.

Sleep overtakes him immediately. (He has never had insomnia, the only nervous tic he has somehow missed. He can fall asleep anywhere, anytime, sometimes against his will. He loves to sleep.) In that sleep he dreams that Kirk Poland tentatively knocks at the door of the bedroom (he would know that knock anywhere) and then enters, ready at last to greet him and discuss important matters of identity . . . but Herovit is not yet ready for that. No. He cannot take on this kind of thing now.

Maybe never. In his dream he leaps from the bed and leans his full weight against the panels to keep, at whatever cost, this confrontation away. He seems to have mixed Kirk up in his mind with a lot of other people, some of them dangerous types.

"Come on," Kirk says, wheedling through the door, speaking with a smooth, level reasonableness, his nifty little hands gesturing away like a mute's. "Come on, let me in; let's discuss this. Let's talk things over reasonably. You've been waiting for a long, long time for this; now we can have it out man to man. You'll like it, you really will. You'll enjoy what I have to say, and you'll learn something too. Why not? Let me in. I won't force you to do a thing against your will that deep inside you don't want to do anyway. I have ideas how you and I can clean up this mess together; I've been turning out this science-fiction crap for twenty years and this could make a man thoughtful. We can change your life and you will never be the same again. Just like you always hoped, if you'll let me in."

"No!" Herovit shouts in the dream, turning his face from the door, inclining his face into the bedframe, feeling the metal curl around his cheeks as he presses wood with his fingernails. "No, I won't have this. I can't take it any more. Just get out of my life, Kirk, let me manage all this myself. I don't want any part of you. Get away from me! I'll resolve this on my own or not at all."

He is afraid that Poland will, if allowed in the bedroom, crash into the walls shrieking accusations, and no matter how he rationalizes this he will never be able to justify his position to the active and evasive Kirk, who has stored up so much hostility, righteous hostility, for so long. Kirk is no Mackenzie. How could he be? He will not be talked out of confrontation, and ultimately Herovit would not have the will. He has caused Kirk suffering and given very little in return. Poland's case is clear.

Dreaming, Herovit decides that if he is only given time enough, perhaps he will think of some way to get Kirk off his back before there is real ugliness. The thing is that he really needs time. Time is the key. He dreams that he awakens and as he does so, it is the start of yet another day.

10

Breaking for some air at midday as he has made his habit (he cannot stand to be in the apartment continuously; not only is the situation untenable, but he feels a loss of vigor, a sense that he might faint if confined to his reeking office), Herovit is again accosted by a beggar in the street. This has happened often. It is one of the West Side beggars with bizarre clothing and a developed, focused philosophy of life which the beggar is eager to disclose.

"Give me all your money," the man says, waving a cane dangerously and placing his glowing teeth in juxtaposition to Herovit's belt—a tiny, menacing beggar this, whose own eyes seem to rake far distances, vast horizons—"Give

me every cent you have or I'll break your head. I don't
have to put up with this forever, you know. There are
limits. Face me, man!"

"I don't have anything," Herovit says. "I only go out
with twenty-five cents during the day." He reaches in a
pocket and offers the quarter to the beggar—the hell with
the newspaper. "Take it," he says. "Fuck it, if you think
that it'll make any difference." Talk their language, get at
their level.

"Don't get metaphysical with me, you stupid son of a
bitch," the beggar says. He backs off two paces, then adjusts his height so that he confronts Herovit at chest level
by straining to his toes. "I don't have to put up with this
libertarian crap. All I get is wise answers from people who
think that they're smart. I want your money."

"I don't have any money," Herovit says. "I really don't;
you have it all." No one seems to be watching this dialogue, which is unusual. On most days, conversations like
this will pick up five to ten amused witnesses making side
comments, but it is a day of clouds with penetrating cold
and perhaps people are too absorbed in their own errands.
There certainly are a good number of them—people, that
is—several hundred passing them by the minute; traffic is
pouring through the intersections and a nice howl of sirens
is rising a few blocks down as an ambulance separates
traffic and moves on its demented way. Could the ambulance be for him? "Just what I offered you, that's all there
is; take it or leave it." He is tired of these West Side beggars, who are more and more defiant nowadays, although
the problem, he understands from the papers, is even
worse in the Village. Mack Miller would not have to put

up with this shit. He would shoot the beggar—all of the beggars—dead as a necessary action. "Excuse me," Herovit says, thinking of what Mack would make of the West Side, and moves to push himself through all of this.

"Not so fast, friend." The beggar uses his cane to give Herovit a warning tap on the instep, then raises it to threaten his forehead. "Just stay in place until we arrive at a solution." Looking at him in this fashion, Herovit comes to understand that the beggar is quite demented, but for all of that no coincidence, no, indeed: he surely must be a symbolic figure. The beggar is an outward extension of all the forces which have made Herovit's life so recently intolerable, a pure abstraction equipped with cane, which cane bears down dangerously toward his skull and then at the last instant—like a sudden royalty check in the mail staving off another dispossess—swings out of track and clatters to the sidewalk. The beggar looks at it with disgust. "Everything," he says, his assurance seeming to dwindle. "I want everything you've got."

"No," Herovit says. "I won't do it, I won't." He dodges to a side. Mack Miller would not be caught evading. Mack Miller would have long since lost his temper; if this were an alien planet and the filthy beggar a native, Mack would have attacked the creature straight on, with weaponry or even fists, and the alien would have slid from his path, mumbling, dissolved. But Herovit is not Mack. He must remember this. The courses which Mack finds so easy to take are simply not, well, *reasonable* when applied to the daily order of Manhattan's West Side. "I won't give you anything now, you see, and you could have had a quarter," he says and bolts toward freedom, moving thus to a small area between a subway kiosk and newsstand where several scraps of old paper twirl absently in the freshening breezes of a bus. "It isn't fair," Herovit mumbles. "It isn't right, it shouldn't be this way."

"What isn't fair?" the beggar shouts, pursuing. "What are you talking about anyway?" Herovit does not know whether the creature is determined or merely making a gesture for the hell of it, but as the voice fades and ripples, he gathers that the beggar is running out of his class. "Everything's fair if you make it so! This is your life. We make the world! Cheap bastard son of a bitch, you should go to hell."

"Go to hell yourself," Herovit says. "Just fuck off," but he says this very quietly, not wanting to further antagonize the beggar, who is obviously sensitive. (Herovit has already given more pain than he can really bear in his unfortunate condition, and anyway, he can imagine what the impact of the cane would be if flung squarely toward the back of a skull.) "Not that I mean it personally, of course; in the impersonal sense we're all *in* hell," he whispers in penance and lunges into Broadway. He gets across the street without incident.

He thinks he hears the beggar still cursing, but when he risks turning at last, now across the street, peering through the haze of traffic and pedestrians, Herovit does not see him. Now with distance established, he realizes that he wanted to see the man, inspect the source of the confrontation, possibly even try to grasp the creature from a newer and more meaningful perspective when aided by

distance ... but no, the man is gone. Merged into land-
scape, like some of Mack Miller's more difficult antagonists.

Herovit reaches in a pocket and finds without surprise
that the bills in the left rear are gone. Thirty-five dollars
or so, his escape money if he ever gets to the point where
he must dive into a furnished room and inaugurate divorce proceedings. "Goddamn it," he says, "they can't do
this to me."

"You see what I mean?" Kirk Poland says. He leans
easily against a lamppost and twirls one leg behind the
other, a picture of ease and confidence as he deftly lights
a cigarette. "Do you understand what I've been trying to
get over to you, Jonathan?" He winks and his complexion
shifts, taking on the color of the post. "You've got to see,"
he says. His tone is as reasonable as would befit any author
of ninety-two published novels. "You're incapable of managing your life. You've lost control, you can no longer
assume responsibility, and I'm here to tell you that it must
stop." Kirk blends in well with Broadway. A certain shab-
biness which has always been at the rim of his personality
works in convincingly against the background.

"Come on," Kirk says, reaching toward him, "let's make
a little agreement now and be done with it. You don't want
to go back to the house and face that crap all over again,
do you?"

Herovit backs away with a shriek. The hell with what
people will think of him; anyway people in Manhattan do
not think, this being their only salvation. He turns and
runs down the full length of Broadway, no longer con-

cerned with his thirty-five dollars. "Please," he is babbling, "please, please, please, give me a break, will you?" Pedestrians turn to look at this fleeing Herovit as if he were a miracle, mingled awe and suspicion on their faces, their hands deep into their pockets to protect folding money. Who knows what guises the beggars are taking now? Who knows what he might, on an impulse, do to any of them?

He accelerates.

11

Finishing off page forty-six he decides that he cannot take this any longer. No matter what the penalty he must vault past the situation, seize some breasts. In easy stages he moves back from the desk, then stands, flexing his buttocks. Lower back syndrome. Herovit has had instances of lower back pain increasing in severity and duration over many years but he cannot really afford an orthopedic survey and has an ancient horror of chiropractors whom he takes to be the science-fiction writers of the medical profession.

"Take that," Mack Miller then shouted triumphantly and leaveled the alien yet again with three steady spurts from the laser fire. At last he had penetrated the mystery of the beast's invulnerability, it responded to thought waves, being sensitive to telepathy as he should have

known from the start and if he broadcast
hatred at it along with the laser fire it
would crumple. Their sensitivity then
would be their destruction . . . if mack
only could bring the word to lies before him and
ends the page; as he scans it quickly, routinely, he thinks
that he really will have to do something about this. All of
it seems vaguely ungrammatical, like the babblings of
some kind of idiot, and it is not even maintained in character in the bargain. This page at least should go through the
typewriter again tomorrow, he knows.

But he tries never to revise. It was an old policy settled
from the beginning. Once you started revising there was
just no end to any of it: first it was a line here or there, then
a paragraph or shred of dialogue that didn't quite work;
soon you were up to whole scenes that didn't work, and in
no time at all, like old Jack Craggings, if you got deep into
the revision question, you might never be able to write
new stuff again. Hunks of novels and short stories, like
dismembered limbs, would be fed through the typewriter
over and again and nothing would ever be right. That was
the problem once you started looking at this stuff critically:
it *never* could be right; it was already rotten to the bottom. Standing there looking at his words crawling around
the page, Herovit seems to recollect hundreds, maybe
thousands, of pulp writers stretching back to antiquity—
or at least to the mid-1920's—who had been brought to
their finish by a belated instinct for revision and now stood
(or lay) mute, their voices not to say their incomes vanished to be unrecovered.

Never revise, he mutters, an old credo. *It doesn't make any difference; the people who read this crap wouldn't know a literate sentence from an illiterate one, and come to think of it, kid, neither would you.* He stumbles through the office door in vague pursuit of his wife.

Their schedules interchange, if never quite mesh. Tonight it has been she who went to bed early while he has stayed in the office to work Mack Miller through, lunge through at least a hundred pages and get the novel well in hand. ("That's great," Janice had said. "I think that you should definitely work through the night and all day tomorrow—just like the old days—so that you can finish it up, and then you can go to bed for a couple of days straight. I won't bother you, I promise, and it's a good plan. I mean, I won't feel deprived of your companionship or throw it up to you that I'm being squeezed out of your life, and that is a definite promise.") Here it is only midnight, and all he has accomplished is five pages. *Five pages! In three hours!* Where are the hacks of yesteryear? Enough, enough of this: he really has to get hold of himself once and for all, no kidding, because he sees what is happening and it is not pleasant. In the bedroom, through the hiss of steam, the sound of urban rains now pelting their West 80th Street windows, he sees Janice curled on her side of the bed, her pillow characteristically bunched around, her body convulsed in that strange position which for her has always been the access to sleep . . . and feels pity. Come in teeming with vengeance just to collapse into pity. What can one do?

"Hello," he says. He sits on the edge of the bed, touches

her lightly. She is naked as she usually is (in the early years of their marriage he had thought this unbearably sensual; now he can see it only as a taunt), and moves under his touch, groans—an uneasy sleeper, this one, but single-minded in her journey.

"Hello," he tries again and releases her. He stands, begins to pull off bits and pieces of his own clothing. Tonight he will have his way with her one way or the other; nothing can stop him. It has been a week since their last copulation (manic, he still counts). Now he is seized by an excitement which may stem only from rage or despair, but so much the better for her, so much the worse for him since he will come quickly. Janice has always been most cooperative when she knows that he will finish without work; she has an uncanny ability (do all women? the ones he has been with do) to time his movements and know exactly where he is while she, for Herovit at least, is a mystery.

He stands in the center of his discarded clothing, flexing and preparing himself for the task like a Surveyman; then like an entire Team avenging an almost-forgotten (but only by Headquarters) alien injury, he flings himself upon her and wildly begins to make the motions of generation. Do it fast and she may not notice. At times she has had this complaint.

But Janice is bolt awake and struggling under him. She must have been feigning sleep after all, this cunning bitch. "What are you doing?" she says. "What the hell do you think you're *up* to? Is this real? Is this something really true?" but he will not be denied by her complaints, not at this instant. His desire has restored him and somehow he will become the man that he was.

He forces penetration while working frantically with her breasts. His other hand he uses to alternately support himself and grab at her chin, cup it, draw her face to his. He will not be denied, not now, not any more; he is Herovit Transmorgrified (for the night anyway), and there are limits to what he can put up with—a published writer, a leading professional in his field. Mack Miller would not take any of her resistance, he reminds himself, thinking of old Mack, telling himself again as he must know that Mack Miller's actual sex life is, of course, a mystery. He oozes inside her, growing. "Come on," he says, breathing this into her lips. "Come on, damn it, I'm entitled to a little consideration, aren't I? I work hard, I do what I can for you, you can't hold me off forever." This is most likely not the right approach. You are supposed to be tender; at least this is what most manuals advise. But Herovit does not feel tender. It has been a day of enormous frustration. He remembers the beggar. Would he have taken this? Like hell he would have—that is the only answer.

"Stop it," Janice says, feeling him inside her. "Now just stop that, you must stop!" but not shouting because (he knows shrewdly) she does not want to wake the baby. At all costs she will not awaken the child, and with his new slyness, Herovit goes right down to the center and sees that this is the key to union. He can do anything he wants because sooner or later she will calculate that it is easier to deal with him than with the child. He digs into her, feeling his own pulsations against her walls, and reaches around to encircle a nipple. He could try to excite her there with his mouth, he supposes. Oh no, scratch that: she has said that since the child she has lost all feeling in that area and finds it, in fact, painful. Oh well. Concentrate on the genital. Be a man. Grow up.

He eases up her pathways, touching familiar tubers and tendrils in greeting as he surges onward. An unexpected responsiveness in her taking glides him up all the way, and he wonders whether she is merely denying passion which lies waiting for him at this end. Or then again what he takes to be invitation may be only slackness; he does not know much gynecology. "I'm entitled to this," he groans encouragingly, locked deep in the motions of intercourse. "You know I'm entitled, it's my right, you can't just take something like this away." This is not the right approach either, but surely he has a point—doesn't he? *Consider my position,* he advises the blankets which lie rumpled bleakly under him. *You have to admit looked at objectively that I have an argument.* He feels her fingernails then against his cheeks. How much of this does a man have to take?

"You're hurting me, Jonathan," she says—at least using his proper name, which is a start. "You've got to stop hurting me now, please, now, please," but it is impossible to stop and how well she must know it. He feels his orgasm begin to overtake him like rocket fire. Long beams of power shuttle in and out of his groin, moving up to his stomach, and he emits an *Aah* of mingled power and submission as almost unaware of himself he spills into her cleanly.

That was fast. Well, he unloaded anyway. He puts his mouth to her shoulder, exposes teeth to bite, and then disengages, feeling even through the narcotherapy of sex her fingernails come more severely into his cheekbones. She does not want him to show postcoital affection, it would seem.

"What the hell do you think you're doing anyway?" he says weakly as he collapses to her side. "What is going on here? Is that conduct? Is that the right sort of thing?"

"Stay away from me," she mutters. "Just stay *away*," and so he rolls to his side of the bed, closing his eyes with the motion. Better not to fight about this now (and at least he got his rocks off), he thinks, feeling small waves of dislocation and pain. He heaves back at her, one hip against her foot, his appendix lying dangerously close to her small pointed knee, and he turns in little wandering rivulets to look up at the ceiling, his hand flat against her. Oh boy.

He stares at the ceiling in a position of perfect receptivity, waiting now to hear anything she might say. Whatever it is, he will have the answers. He wants her to speak. Let her say one thing and he will demolish her, because he has the answers. His position is justifiable; she has no defense. Furthermore, even in his need, he tried to give her a good time. It was hardly his fault if she would not participate. The record is clear. Let them take a look at that record. All of them. All the sons of bitches.

He waits and waits; she says nothing. One word and he would have it all before her. But silence. "Well," he says finally, "don't you have a thing to say? Nothing at all?"

She says nothing. She says nothing; he lies there poised waiting for the words that will knife him open and enable him to send the truth like a flood upon her, but she says nothing. From too much alertness he feels quickly diluted toward fatigue. His eyes close, his head lolls into the pillow; detumescent at last, he slides against himself.

She is silent.

Herovit, hunched against the night, sleeps.

12

"I wouldn't let her get away with it," Kirk says, smiling, "not if I were in your position. You just don't know how to handle this kind of a situation." He rubs his hands, leans forward in a confidential manner. "And it's so simple if you only know what to do; the problem could be solved in a minute. Why don't you give me a shot at it, eh? You must admit that you've pretty much reached the end of your devices."

"Oh, shut up," Herovit says, "just shut up and let me be," but he does not know if he is arguing with Kirk or only asking for his sympathy while he tries to buy some time. The trouble is, how much sympathy can Kirk, the creator of the Survey Team, really have?

13

Herovit is visited unexpectedly by his old collaborator Mitchell Wilk (pseudonym: Dan Robinson). They had not done *that* much collaboration—just a few stories for Steele here and there—but Herovit, who has always been lonely and finds it difficult to establish relationships, would prefer to think of Wilk as a collaborator rather than as just another struggling member of the long-disbanded S-F Guild of the 1950's, who would just as soon knife him as sit down to work on a story.

Wilk, who somehow managed to get a job in the department of English of mediocre Lancastrian University some time ago and has not done any writing for more than a decade, has a strange way of recurring in Herovit's existence. Herovit will hear nothing from the man for years (Wilk never writes letters, refusing to furnish free copy to anyone) and then, as on this morning, he will present himself to whatever new aspect Herovit's life has taken with the air of taking up an interrupted conversation three minutes later. All of this is done with such arrogance and assurance that one can hardly get mad at old Wilk; it is nothing personal, just that like some science-fiction writers, Wilk has never outgrown the habit of looking at life as if it were something he had slipped into one of his novels to bulk out the wordage, Herovit then being a minor but important character in the latest Dan Robinson work.

"I do see," Wilk says, ducking his bald head to come through the low frame of the apartment door, "I do see what's happening now." He nods at Janice and the baby in the living room and then strides powerfully behind Herovit to his office, shaking his head, fondling his beard with the same infuriating kind of self-satisfaction which has remained as intact as some complex loathing Herovit feels toward himself. "I understand this situation," Wilk says, closing the door firmly. "It looks like a child, yes? And the devastating effect which the child would have upon a marriage at your age along with the effects on the sex life. Very sad. Sad! Your work has declined severely, Jonathan. I've been watching it sink for years now, and the stuff I've looked over recently looks absolutely dreadful. Of course I do very little reading nowadays, but for old time's sake I try to see how my friends are doing. Disgraceful, old man! How long can you keep this up?"

"Who cares?" Herovit says rather stiffly. Wilk has always had this ability to put him on the defensive; even while they were collaborating, Herovit was doing eighty percent of the first drafts and all of the finished (as he recollects it) and yet somehow he felt that he had to *apologize* to Wilk for gumming up the work. "You have no right to say this to me. What right do you have to come into my apartment and start talking to me in this way?" His voice sounds faintly European, shrill and effeminate to his ears.

He must face this: Wilk has never brought out the best in anybody Herovit knew.

"Anything goes between old friends, Jonathan. What I say I say for your own good; your condition is a source of real distress to me." Wilk has worked his beard down to a small goatee, Herovit notices, and seems to have cultivated a kind of academic simper which makes him even more infuriating. Underneath all of this, however, and under whatever guise is the same old Mitchell Wilk: a barely compensated alcoholic who during the late fifties and early sixties produced a series of novelettes and short stories for *Thrilling* which, although received as devastating social satire, were actually poorly transmuted portraits of Wilk's family and friends, quite libelous if anyone had had the time or money to sue. Most of these stories were written by Wilk in his underwear in a furnished apartment, his typewriter framed by bottles of gin and obscene notes which Wilk would type to himself during incessant blocks, begging him not to let up now. (*How can you do this to me, you bastard?* the notes would say, *You know we need the money.*)

Herovit thus has never been able to disentangle his truest opinions of the work from that image, although he realizes that in certain areas Wilk is considered to be one of the masters and has a fine, if limited, reputation. He has always made the best-of-the-year anthologies, Herovit never, and Wilk has not been gracious about this. ("Level seeks its level," he has cautioned Herovit. "It stands to reason that even in this miserable mud puddle I would avoid the stagnant waters.") Now, although this creature does not even have a high school diploma, he has somehow found long-term employment as a Visiting Professor of Creative Writing and Fantasy which is not, any way you look at it, too bad.

"I don't think that you should carry on this way," Herovit finishes sullenly and stands with hands on hips, elbows poking the wall, while Wilk surveys the office. "After all, we came out of the same factories, and I find your attitude snide and nasty."

Wilk, immaculate as always recently, adjusts his tie, flicks off a speck of dust and stoops over the typewriter to read the completed page 46 of *Survey Sirius,* still inserted. He moves his shoulders in random gestures, groans. "This is terrible, Jonathan," he says after a short, quiet interval. "Why, this is the worst thing I've ever seen. I wouldn't even dignify it by calling it self-parody. Have you really deteriorated this much? Or perhaps this is some kind of a joke for a letter column. I thought that I could help straighten you out but now, looking at this, I'm at a complete loss. What can I say to you? It hurts me to read this. The syntax alone is frightening."

"It's a new novel," Herovit says unhappily, "an important one for a new publisher. It's just a first draft, coming out kind of sloppy, and has to be run through three or four more times before it starts to get into shape. I've taken to very careful, thorough rewrites since you've last known me." No matter what Wilk says to him, how vituperative his old friend becomes, Herovit always winds up sullen and apologetic. It stems, he supposes, from a basic sense of inferiority which he will never overcome even though he himself has never found Wilk that convincing a writer. "It's a contract novel. I mean, I've already been paid for the portion; this isn't speculative work. It's a money book. They thought enough of me to put a thousand down. How much have you been making from portions recently?"

"But it's horrible, Jonathan! Surely you must be able to tell this yourself; I know you haven't gone down that far, have you? No one could go to this level without at least knowing it. Why, the stuff of yours I've been looking at here and there is awful, but this, my old friend, *this*—" Wilk stops and looks at the ceiling, the floor, the typewriter, the scotch bottle, all of these aspects of Herovit's life as if they, not he, could provide an explanation. "I guess you'd better give me a drink. That will relieve the shock and then we can discuss this quietly."

"I thought you were off the stuff. That's the word you were passing around."

"I recur in your life at many stages, many cycles, my friend. Now you see me, as they say, and now you don't. Call it a study of sea change, confluence, the mystery of cyclical return and refurbishment, or then again it is the academic overlay here which is absolutely critical. Pervasive. Persuasive." Wilk belches, a sound like a hollow gunshot. "I am back onto the stuff, Jonathan. It is a sea change; there are worse things," he says.

He takes the bottle, holds it for a moment while he examines the label ("Cheap stuff, but then again I remember how it was in my free-lancing days"), and then puts the bottle to his lips, where he puts away a fair quantity of scotch in a series of choking swallows, much like a man drinking from a beer can. "Jesus Christ," Wilk says, then puts down the bottle with a clatter next to the typewriter and wipes his goatee with a handkerchief shaken down from a cuff. "You've got to get hold of yourself if you don't want to break down completely. That isn't bad booze, by the way; it's all the same, you know, they just line up once a year in Scotland and help themselves from the same vat. Now, as you should know, I haven't written a word in ten years, thank God, and I only hope this block is permanent, but if I were to do so, if I were *forced,* if it were life or death, I know that I could reach up at least *around* my established standard. I hold onto that kind of pride and basic self-confidence. On the other hand, I read these pages and I see a man wallowing in the mire, perhaps enjoying the very specter of his own degradation, and this saddens me greatly because I remember you as a man with great pride."

"All right," Herovit says, "enough. I don't want to hear any more of this, you have no idea what I'm going through." Outside, Natalie begins to cry, Janice to swear at her. Midmorning, the usual. The sounds thread in and out of his office like a surgical knot, tighten around his psyche. "Oh God," he says unconsciously, "I just don't think that I can stand this."

Wilk listens to the sound for a little while, then smiles and fondles the bottle of scotch again. "I've been intolerant. I said it when I came in; I should have made the connection. Pressures, Jonathan, these I can understand. The tensions accruing here would have to unman a satyr.

I'll take that into account, and you have my sympathy, rest assured."

He gives Herovit a rather horrid wink and pokes him. "Sex life not too good, is that it? Generally after the first child they don't want to be touched for a long time. You remember Margaret, my first wife—well, she was hot as hell but I couldn't get *near* her for weeks after she came out of the hospital. And then too Janice is a little on the old side. Not a *hag,* of course—I don't mean to insult either of you—but my calculations are that she's close to forty anyway—"

"Now listen here," Herovit says. His voice is shaking a little; he had better cut this out. "What the hell do you want anyway, Wilk? I haven't seen you in years but you come into my home, insult my work, start going into highly personal material ... " He stops, baffled. There must be something he had meant to say to Wilk but now he cannot quite think of it. The trouble is that he agrees with most of what he has heard.

"Ah, come now," Wilk says, probably seeing this, laughing offhandedly as he shrugs his shoulders in his ticlike way and wipes the nose of the bottle with a palm. Mitch certainly had a good collection of nervous habits. *Stasis is not my bag,* he had said once. "Come, relax, we're all old friends and thieves together; there's no reason for you to take this very dangerous loose attitude. In the bargain, Jonathan, I haven't come here to insult your work at all. That was just a side issue, although you must admit that it's getting pretty bad and no one asked you to leave it right out there in the typewriter for everyone to see; that is your own masochism. I've come here to do you some real good and in my official capacity. What you really need is a long rest and possibly a divorce—if you want to know."

"I don't need a long rest."

"And the divorce? You have nothing to say about the divorce?"

"Leave me alone, please. I could use a little understanding, that's all," Herovit says, absorbing a small cannonade of pokes in the rib cage from Wilk's demented elbow. "Not that I'd get any from you."

"But you do have understanding! I've sized up the situation completely."

"I'm going to order you out of here, is what I'm going to do, and put down that goddamned scotch bottle."

"No matter," Wilk says abruptly, holding the bottle against his stomach, his nostrils whitening. "No matter if that's going to be your attitude. I'll refuse to discuss your professional problems any further if that's the way you want it. No, as I say, I'm here in an official capacity."

"To insult me?"

"Only marginally. I'm in my role as visiting adviser and lecturer in English, and now head of the new credit science-fiction program," Wilk says with a trace of smugness. "We're going to have a seminar week starting next Monday, and I'm inviting you."

"Inviting me for what? I don't think that I understand."

"I'm inviting you to the seminar, Jonathan! Now don't be so obtuse. Your writings don't show brain damage, just a complete collapse of technical facility and of a sense of self-worth. Science fiction is very big in the academic world now; more and more theses and courses are being given on it every year because of the overuse of Henry James, and people like you and me—simple hacks, Jonathan!—are in a position of unparalleled opportunity." Wilk stops and takes a long, suckling drink from the scotch bottle, then holds it into his belly as he continues. Infantile behavior, Herovit supposes, but then who is he, who is anyone in the field, to comment on that? "Starting Monday there's going to be a full program on science fiction. We're having a series of lectures, presentations, convocations and cocktail parties. Cocktail parties! Discussions of modern science fiction at all of these. Just to keep them on the budget."

"It sounds wonderful."

"It is wonderful. Now in order to float this little academic boondoggle, which incidentally is *completely* underwritten by two of the largest research foundations you could imagine, we need a writer or two in attendance. We hope that writer will be you."

"That's fantastic," Herovit says. The baby should have stopped crying by now, but oddly she has not. The shrieks, in fact, have turned blood red; obviously a diaper is being changed. "Give me that bottle, damn it," he says angrily to Wilk and wrestles it away, then after an instant of hesitation, puts it to his own mouth and drinks. So maybe the guy has syphilis. So, so what? He deserves a drink, doesn't he?

"Of course this is an academic affair, you know," Wilk says confidentially, his nose flaring as it apprehends the depth and peculiar solidity of Natalie's screams, "and I

don't think that they'll be able to do much better than
cover moderate expenses, but there should be at least a
hundred-dollar honorarium and I know you can use it.
And the truly important thing is that the ass on campus,
the *ass* is fantastic. Nowadays they call it cunt, Jonathan,
but we're locked back in a simpler time and I'll always
think of it as ass, forgive me. You have no idea what's been
happening in the last ten years unless you get back to
college and see what's walking around there nowadays."

"You never even went to college."

"Who cares? They all have a contempt for the educa-
tional process and want to tear it down anyway. Do you
know that they like to fuck? I mean, they really like it!"

Mack Miller would not have to put up with this shit.
Mack Miller would not have to stand in his own office, his
own control room, and listen to some balding, bearded
fool of a washed-up hack bait him and then start teasing.
Mack would have seized a weapon a long time ago and
cleared out the invader. But the thought of the ass that
likes to fuck, like the remote strains of departed music,
touches Herovit. Despising himself, he moves closer, holding the bottle like a steering wheel. "That's what I read,"
he says hoarsely, "in the newsmagazines and like that."

"And it's true. For once the media haven't lied to us!
They think it's their moral *duty* to screw, is what it is,
because that's the modal point of creating a relationship,
and it means nothing to them. They're happy to do it!
They'll call anything a relationship if it gives them an
excuse. Oh God, my God," Wilk says, seizing the bottle
and inhaling another cautious sip, his face glowing and

enlarging in the dim light as if alcohol can alter its proportions, "I cannot properly convey to you what is going on down there. You'll come and see it and then you'll know what I mean. Consider it a favor from an old friend that may change your life."

"A hundred dollars? That's really the best that they can do for someone?"

"You're a hack," Wilk says with sudden rage. He always was labile that way, his moods shifting from minute to minute depending upon his word count or anticipations for the evening. "That's always been your problem. Your sights, the sights of all of us in the guild, were so low. A penny a word, two, four cents a word, go to the fifteen-hundred-dollar markets and call it quits. Everything on the front end—you'd sell all rights to anything for an extra two hundred because all you ever understood were nickels and dimes. All of us were the same way back then, but I've grown and changed and you haven't. You're almost forty, man! Don't you know that it's all going to end pretty soon? You're talking about a hundred dollars, trying to squeeze out another twenty or some such, and I'm standing here trying to offer you a week, such a week as . . ." Wilk stops, swallows, fondles his goatee, slams the bottle on the desk. It would seem that the immaculate grooming and high urbanity with which he entered the apartment may have been a bit fraudulent; in any event, it is all falling away from him in small pieces. Standing before him is a suggestion of the disheveled, frantic Wilk of fifteen years ago who was convinced that everyone was out to get him and knew that he had to Take Measures.

"I have a good mind to walk out of here," this younger, less tasteful Wilk says, "and to take my offer away with me. I only came by because I thought that you, as one of my oldest and most discreet friends, could *use* something like this in your own life, which incidentally is obviously going to hell if you only had the courage to stand up and admit that you've got the problem. That's the first step in these cases, you know."

"Now wait," Herovit says, thinking of all the ass on or in the campus. "I didn't say I wouldn't go." He looks at and then quickly away from the page in the typewriter. "The only thing is that you're giving me kind of short notice and I have this overdue novel which I really have to finish and deliver."

"Don't finish. Don't deliver. It's awful; you can't hand in stuff like that. Bail out on the contract and let them sue to collect. You and I know that in the history of American letters a publisher never collected a dime on forfeiture clauses. Oh hello, Janice."

The baby squeaks, probably from the position in which she is being held as Janice opens the door, eases a long hand through, then an arm, and finally half her body. The baby then shifts to discontented mews. "Don't ask," Janice says.

"Don't ask what?"

"Ask how I am."

"I didn't ask how you were, Janice," Wilk says. "Not yet anyway."

"If you were going to, you could have when you came in. But you have utter contempt for women, don't you.

They don't matter as people in your little world. You wouldn't even nod."

"I did *so*," Wilk says, veins now pulsing small clots of blue across his cheeks. Obviously not a healthy man. "I nodded the minute I came in. Jonathan and I had some business to discuss which I couldn't delay because otherwise I might forget. You know how forgetful I am, dear."

"Don't call me 'dear.' "

"How long has this been going on, Jonathan?" Wilk asks. "It has an air of permanency."

"You're all the same," Janice says, engrossed in herself. Probably this is something she has worked out at leisure in the living room. "Every last one of you is the same. You all make about six thousand dollars a year after taxes, and you don't even think that women exist except to get on their hands and knees or in some cases on their backs."

Janice is obviously in one of her foulest postnatal moods ever. Given time, Herovit guesses that he could draw Wilk aside and quietly explain the situation to him as Wilk followed it intently. He could tell old Mitch that this thing with Janice was hardly personal, merely her usual resentment of the situation now being tacked onto Wilk, and anyway, this was not a new speech ... but no time for whispered conversations off in the corners (unlike the convention where he had met her, when he had been able to check on her track record and coital possibilities within three minutes while she had stood against a wall, holding a drink and looking at him blandly). No time for conversations now; this is not a convention. Mack Miller would not have to put up with this garbage. Mack would seize a beam and order the bitch out of the control room. *This is real life,* he would have said to her in deadly controlled tones, *and you don't bother a Surveyman when he's working.* A long way from old Mack, however; he is going to have to negotiate this on his own.

"Don't bother him with your lies about college, that's all I ask," Janice says bitterly, "and how wonderful it is to be out there teaching and how the whole sexual morality has changed and how all the coeds are crazy to go down on science-fiction writers. I don't think that he could stand to listen to that. He's so stupid and gullible, he'd probably go out of his mind."

"Give him some credit."

"You have no courtesy. You have no manners. You hate women. I know what you've come here to do and I don't like you at all."

Oh God. There is no dealing with her when she has worked to this pitch, which she seems to do now at least once a week anyway, although so far in the privacy of their bedroom. This is Janice in her mood of Random Accusation—a time when her stream of consciousness can shift with fluent ease through any succession of topics, however disjointed, without ever escaping the common denominator of Herovit's inadequacy. Or, in this case, Wilk's. Natalie stares at Wilk sullenly; Herovit inspects his daughter carefully (except during sex he has not looked at Janice carefully in months) and decides that the effect upon the baby must be indisputably bad. Surely this cannot be the proper environment in which the child should grow. Before she can even articulate, she will have conceived the most utter loathing for science fiction and science-fiction writers.

Come to think of it, Herovit vaguely recalls having dealt with the theme. One of the middle novels. In a subliterate society composed largely of slaves to galactic overlords ruling by fiat, the cunning little Survey Team had succeeded in turning the situation around by planting in the aliens an absolute hatred of their masters. They had become slaves to the Survey Team instead, good slaves. When had he written that? He guesses that it was in 1961 or thereabouts. In 1961 the best way to sell *Tremendous* was to cobble up a good justification of slavery and send it off to Steele with a sincere covering letter saying that you were trying to think the unthinkable through. The bastard.

"It's all right, Janice," Wilk is saying anyway with some ease. He renders an archaic bow and brandishes the scotch bottle, from which he seems to take a final, reluctant sip, winking a goodbye at the bottle. "Jonathan is a fine writer —at least he could have been a fine writer if he hadn't gotten mechanical, and we've just been reliving the old times together. Old times and a smidgen of business, as they say. You must be very proud of him. Through thick and thin he's kept on working, and that's the important thing, isn't it? Would that I had that kind of dedication."

Wilk burps, an unsettled expression moves perilously across his features, and momentarily he seems to lose control over the gross motor functions. Disconcerted—or then he may only be responding to Janice's aggression, which is really quite extreme. Herovit can see this now;

the woman might need a psychiatrist. "I guess I'll be getting along," Wilk says in a tiny voice. "I have a number of other contacts, quite a number, to make in this city, and as much as I'd like to stay around enjoying memories, I'm afraid that I must be getting on."

"Just go. Get out of our lives. Who needs you anyway?" Janice says.

"Well, that's hard to answer at this stage. Who needs any of us, Janice? In any event, being on the university payroll keeps one hopping, and Jonathan, ah, seems to have a novel to finish. I'll be at the Dixie Hotel through tomorrow morning; you can reach me there and confirm acceptance, Jonathan, and then we'll be able to make arrangements."

"Cheap hotel," Janice says. "Cheap writing."

"You'll find that I'm not registered under my real name," Wilk says rather frantically, scratching his scalp, sidling toward the door, jostling Natalie in a panicky fashion as the child sweeps him with a quizzical look. "I thought that it would be best, for various reasons you might understand, to be under a pseudonym. And it was nice to be Dan Robinson again."

"I think I know what you mean."

"You have the same trouble, Jonathan; it's one of the reasons I always felt *simpático*. Kirk Poland, Dan Robinson—half the field is under pseudonyms. Just like you, I was saving my own name for the real work I was going to do some day. Dan Robinson was just for pulp, remember? Well," Wilk says with a sigh, "it's very hard to predict the future, of course."

"You haven't written a thing in years," Janice says, "and

you'll never write again. You're a washed-up, beaten-up old hack who's afraid of women and uses them to work out your hostilities. Like bed boards." She juggles the baby like a bowling ball in the alley. "It took me a long time to understand people like you, but science fiction is full of them. Just full of them, you understand me?"

"Please, Janice," Herovit says helplessly, "you know there's really no need for this and you've got to stop—"

"It's all right," Wilk says. "I mean, I understand, and these little tensions have their own basis." He is now out the office door, backing toward the main exit which he finds by instinct, his hands reaching behind to grasp the knob as he inclines his head in a gesture of sudden humility, fixes his eyes on the dazzling view of bathrooms across the courtyard that is one of the finest features of this apartment. Misdirection, that old Manhattan trick—Wilk must recall it well. He should, having lived here for so many years himself before going on to the university where, for all Herovit knows, he may have done very well. As Wilk says, science fiction is definitely coming up in the academic world, and a man with those credentials might be able to actually make a living, to say nothing of getting respect. And finding ass. That would be a good possibility.

"Goodbye," Wilk says, now easing out the door; "good-bye, goodbye to you," now closing the door. Small locks and tumblers fall into place with an alienated finality. Herovit is then left, still standing in the office, shoulder blades propped to a wall, staring at Janice. For all of Wilk's offered possibilities, they are back where they started. *Did*

I ask for this? he wonders, and reminds himself that the issue was never one of request.

Janice juggles the baby; they stare. He realizes again that they have nothing to say beyond his despair, her spite —all of it terribly depressing. Somewhere in the distance he senses that an audience is murmuring and flicking pages of programs, waiting for the first-act curtain, at last, to fall at this proper time. An old, old fantasy this: since he was twelve Herovit has lived in the dreamlike conviction that his life is a play. A Pulitzer Prize winner to the natives of Uranus or whatever who form an endlessly attentive audience which is, of course, immortal. Unlike him. Maybe this is the third-act curtain if you want to go by the thesis of the well-made play. He hopes not. Still, the production is full of dead spots and small gropings of dialogue as well as uncertainties of characterization which indicate that most of the time this inconsistent playwright simply does not know what the hell he is doing.

"This is impossible," Janice says. "You're bad enough but your friends are worse. I'm losing patience with everything, you fool. Everything!" She looks at the pages spilling from his typewriter, pages to the left and right of him, infinitesimal driplets of scotch from Wilk's departed mouth glistening in the illumination of the tensor lamp, and her eyes bulge, slowly inflate with admonition.

"No," he says helplessly. "No, please—"

"You'd just better not do it. Whatever he wants you to do, you'd better not go along with him, that's all I can say. Your first responsibility is to us, you fucking idiot." She leaves, the child casting a few burbles like small flowers in their wake as Janice closes the office door behind them, then gives it a kick for good measure before she returns to her place in the kitchen. Indoors, Janice is in the kitchen all day unless she is in the converted dining room changing diapers or, both screaming, putting the child in bed.

Delimitation. Yes indeed. His wife's life has been severely narrowed. This often happens to women after their first pregnancy. Maybe things would have worked out better if they had used the occasion of insemination to rent a five-and-a-half room. Even a small house. In Queens or someplace reasonably suburban like Bensonhurst or Borough Park instead of hanging onto the four in the West Eighties because, well, they were covered by the remnants of rent control and it would have been too much trouble to have left.

But then again—and ask Mack Miller about this if there are doubts—it is lives which make circumstance. *Circumstance does not make lives, Mack reminded himself shrewdly.* Strong-willed, independent men would not suffer as Herovit is suffering.

Ah, God. He sits quickly, extends a leg to kick the door more firmly closed, pulls the chair to the desk, and considers what is in his typewriter. "Get those rockets aligned now, men!" Mack said to the crew-slaves, and slowly the great ship shuddered as it shot showers into space, then ground its engines for the launch. Mack felt himself partake of the power of the ship; it was a good feeling to know that you had at your beck and call something so

vast and capable of weaponing such enormous destruction. Not so good. Not good at all; this
is very bad stuff, Wilk was right, and maybe a man *would*
be better off dead than turning out garbage like this for
adolescents, most of whom were afraid of their own erec-
tions and would have to work themselves gradually to a
state where they could function with girls. Not that he
wants to pursue this line any more. It is just all too depressing.

One thing is sure, Herovit thinks—groaning, typing
again (what else is there to do?), putting the shots of
spheres showering ever more sharply into the shimmers of
space—Mack would not put up with this. Neither would
Kirk Poland. Not even Kirk.

Where is that bastard now? "Where are you now, now
that I need you so?" he asks the ceiling, typing away,
plugging at it. No response from Poland. Of course.

The man is a joker; he comes at whim and his offers can
not be taken seriously. If Kirk really cared, he would be
omnipresent; his absence is the answer. Nevertheless,
what if he did turn the whole mess over to Kirk? Would
he even show? It would be just Herovit's luck; he is hal-
lucinating out of severe anxiety reaction, but his Doppelgänger is not even reliable.

"Where were you when I needed you?" he asks the
ceiling absently as screams again fill the kitchen. Not to
think of it. It is only Natalie ... Or then again, is it Janice?

14

That night, closing the door of his office firmly and drunkenly after dinner, he phones Wilk in the desperation and hush of the assassin at the job to say that he has thought the matter over carefully and will appear at the seminar. At the state university. Definitely. Definitely, that is, if his reasonable expenses will be covered in addition to the honorarium, which had better be given to him on acceptance. "For old time's sake," he says hoarsely, "that's why."

"Wonderful, Jonathan!" Wilk screams. His aplomb and arrogance seem to have been recaptured fully by time, if not the distance from Janice. "There was never any doubt in my mind that you'd accept, though it's a little bit late to call, don't you think, old friend?"

"It's only nine."

"That's true but I'm no longer a free-lancer. I haven't been one for so long, you know, and I've gotten used to thinking of the evening as my own time, if you know what I mean. Anyway, I can't guarantee expenses. I can only say that I'll fight for every break, and anyway I'll drive you down myself on Sunday, so what are the expenses? You'll have a lovely couple of days and you'll get laid a lot and that's the really important thing, isn't it? Isn't it, my boy?" Wilk says, babbling, amiable, confidential, hysteric; adding that he will be giving Herovit a call in a few days just to confirm these arrangements and set a definite time for the trip, he hangs up on him.

Herovit thinks that he may have heard giggling in the background throughout this. Wilk, the old bastard, is definitely getting laid by something Manhattanite and sensual, but Herovit reminds himself that he will no longer be overtaken by erotic fantasies. This must stay beyond him; he does not even know if adultery is within his immediate means. He is thirty-seven years old, married, a father; there is a novel he must finish—be reasonable already.

He puts down the phone quietly then, looking at page forty-eight. At least he is that far; they cannot take this away from him, the sons of bitches. If he dies of a stroke right now, this instant, sitting at this desk, blinking and trying to resist yet another drink, they will have to say that he was the author of ninety-two novels and forty-eight pages. He has gone this far. As executor, Mackenzie could pick up these forty-eight and farm them out to another of his hacks for the completion, but Herovit's name would have to appear on the book. No one thinks that he can do it but he can: he has fifteen thousand words done. Well, no —more like ten thousand with the wide margins and special tricks he has learned about indentation, but anyway, they *look* like fifteen and if he can play tricks, so can the publisher. Their typographers could probably bulk these up to seventy-five. He has seen it done.

Survey Team is in a monumental spot. The aliens have

turned out to be sufferers from a contagious mental illness. They can project paranoia and despair at the Earthmen at will, and Mack Miller is therefore floundering. His normal cheer is interwoven with vague flashes of depression and nausea; his strong brown hands tremble as he tries to push control levers.

All right, so he has used the device already. So he has to get his ideas from somewhere, doesn't he? And self-plagiarism puts him in no legal trouble. After ninety-two novels what do the bastards expect anyway? He is doing the best he can. Balzac was supposed to have done a lot of books, and Dickens of course, but in modern times very few people have written more than fifty novels, and almost all of them are pornographers, who do not count. Pornography is simple-minded; anyone can write a hundred pornographic novels through the simple and timeless extension of limbs and sensations, but the science-fiction writer, who must create a universe from scratch (Herovit tells himself proudly), is a serious and inventive artist. Most of the people with whom he is competing are around the thirty- or forty-novel mark, with only a couple out there ahead of him, both of them much older. Fifty and fifty-five. Tom Walker and John Sands, and John's output must be down to five or six books a year now; *he* cannot take it any more.

No, no: he has a perfect right to repeat himself, and since there is a new generation of readers coming into the field—a ninety-percent complete turnover every three years, the librarians say—what the hell does he have to feel guilty about? Most of the editors understood you and didn't ask too much as long as you came in around the deadlines; it was only stupid bastards like this H. Smythe at Branham who could get you into trouble, but if they wanted to stay around the field they would learn too. They would learn that standards had to be flexible and that if you wanted a popular writer you had to allow him to write once again the things which made him so popular.

Wilk is getting laid. He always had that gift, the bastard; he is getting laid right this minute. It has never been any other way; in any situation, be it convention or barroom, Wilk has always been able to dig up one of his vague, sensual, New York-type girls to lay. He could whisk them right out of the premises and into one of the succession of hotel rooms he used for this, where over and over again he would enter them. Herovit knows exactly how it must have been for Wilk—the contemptible ease of it, the submersion of flesh; he must cut this out and do some writing. One of the responsibilities of the commercial writer was to please the editors and readers, but how can he please them if he is going to sit and think about Wilk being laid? What does he care about Wilk? All of this happened a long time ago and Wilk might have turned into a homosexual in the interim—why not? Decades did strange things to people; he could be a roaring fag. But even if he were, Herovit thinks, he would *still* manage to carry out the vaguest and most sensual piece of ass from the room.

No. Detach himself, remain cold, get this stupid novel out before Branham cancels him out and his agent drops him in disgrace with another open letter to the field. (When he chooses to drop a client, Mackenzie likes to

advise fan magazines through long, raving letters of con-
demnation, another good reason not to leave the grand old
man or not to get near him in the first place.) Lurching
to his feet, Mack took a firmer hold on the
big laser, then looked around him quizzi-
cally at the surfaces of the planet on
which he had just landed. It was a good
planet, a friendly planet. The atmo-
spheric content was just right, the
fields looked like earth-type grass, and
Mack could imagine how they would feel
against his bare feet, the almost sensual
touch of the blades as they brushed
against him, curling in between the pockets of his toes. So why was it so irre-
trievably hostile to him, this planet?
Why did he feel that he was pursued by constant menace? Why was he so depressed and
what could he do about it?

Wilk and the girl were giggling in bed now. His hands
would be on her breasts, the nipples tentatively rising into
his palms, her lips paying small tribute against his as he
told her stories about the old Herovit to make her hot. Old
Herovit had been a whirlwind in his younger days, Wilk
was saying: seventeen novels in one year, and a record for
novel-writing of three days flat. No deadline, no conditions
(other than merit) could defy him, and yet here he was,
thirty-seven years old and fallen on grim times ... grim-
mer still because he could have gotten an easy job in the
academy if he had only anticipated and latched onto the

science-fiction boom. But no such luck for Herovit, Wilk was saying as he nudged the girl toward renewed passion with one devastating touch of his genitals, Herovit's sense of timing for all those years had been absolutely abominable. He had gotten involved with Steele just when Steele was beginning to lose favor among the leaders of the field, he had dived into paperback writing when the field was just beginning to find hardcover outlets, he had married a girl who probably went down for the troops, and then he had indulged in this last insanity of impregnating that girl, now an aging wife of thirty-five. Seed and spawn indeed; Herovit's generations will voyage among the stars as well, but was it really worth it? Wilk waits for the girl to answer but she says nothing, being too busily at work on Wilk's trapped but delighted organ.

Now he really must stop this. Enough of it. This constant cycle of self-hatred, pity and constructs of humiliation must end. Who cares? What does he have to gain? And besides that it is all imagining; Wilk could not care less. If he is getting laid, he is certainly not thinking of Herovit; if he is not, he is worrying about how he might. Who cares? Who cares about the sorrows of Herovit. He cannot take himself seriously; why would Wilk?

No. He has dedicated his life and ninety-two novels to the principle that the reader is entitled to a little relaxation, a little recreation, some escapist adventure in the breaks, and making Mack Miller introspective or doom-filled would certainly not have been the way into the serial market. Wilk always had it easy. There are only two kinds of men in the world, those who have it easy and those who do not, and Wilk—that son of a bitch—gets laid as easily as Herovit gets drunk. Face it. Face the truth of relations.

Why was he so depressed? Mack asked himself again. He looked around at the new spaces which surrounded him, telling himself of all the good things in his life to counteract the strange unhappiness. He was a member of the Survey Team, in magnificent health, with a lifetime of adventure and accomplishment behind him and still he was relatively young. Everything lay ahead, the conquests of the galaxies.

Yet at this moment Mack Miller found himself so depressed that uncharacteristically he could cry. He had never felt this way before in his entire life he did not think. Why did Wilk get everything? At the beginning, in the guild they had all been the same. Fools, hacks, yet brothers together. Now Wilk was in one room and Herovit was in another. It was not fair. There was some terrible inequity here.

"The hell with everything," Mack wanted to say, watching the laser dangling uselessly from his fingers. He wondered if he would ever use it again, and a flare of nostalgia lit his mind. "The hell with the Survey Team, the hell with exploring new worlds. The hell with rocket ships and lasers. It is all lies

and stupidity; I accomplished nothing. I
have wasted my life believing in machinery and have found at the end the same
useless sadness of the flesh. I want
something simple and basic now, something permanent and timeless. Respite,
an end to struggle and an end—unthinka-
bly—of the Survey Team itself. Stupid
bastards, all of them." This is what Mack
wanted to say.

And then he realized he had said it.

And knowing that, he said it again, fondling his weaponry, incalculably depressed, listening to the words he was
uttering with disbelief. For the first
time in his life he hardly knew what he
wanted to do, which was a very unusual
situation because Mack always knew what
he wanted to do.

Didn't he? Didn't certainty inform his
every step? No, this was not like him, really not like him at all. He would have to
take measures against these aliens, and
yet he did not know if he had the strength.
Or if anything mattered.

Herovit stops. Page fifty will have to take care of itself
for now. Dreamlike, he picks up the phone, the fumes of
his inebriation coming back from the mouthpiece in thick,
slow waves. He dials Wilk's hotel again. The switchboard
puts him through to the room. A woman answers. Angrily.

"This is Jonathan," he says, "Jonathan Herovit. I want to talk to Mitchell again."

"What's wrong with you?"

"That's none of your business."

"You just call any time? Haven't you got any sense of decency?"

"Put me through."

"Mitchell," the girl says, "this Herovit wants to talk to you again." A sultry, self-engrossed New York voice, this one, probably pouring from a mouth just involved in skillful fellatio and mumbled assurances of love. How much more of this can he take? Really, he is pushing himself to the edge. *Stop it,* Herovit cautions himself, closing his eyes. *Think only of immediacies.*

"Well, Jonathan," Wilk says coming on after a long pause. He must have been adjusting his genitals, or at least their position. Herovit is sure that fornication must continue; he thinks he hears grunts. "What is it? What do you want? This is really a little ridiculous, you know, calling me twice at this hour after our talk."

"I'm sorry."

"Don't be sorry. Just tell me what it is. What do you want?"

"I don't know. I just don't *know.*"

"You're not backing out on me this time, are you? I hope not, but this is not, uh, the time to discuss things, Jonathan, if you follow what I'm saying. I mean, I can't persuade you to fix up your life at this—oh, my God—this time."

The girl's voice shrieks again. Herovit thinks he hears the rustle of sheets covering breasts, breasts sliding to a new position. "Ah," Wilk says. "Ah, my God. Cut this short, will you?"

"I can't stand this any more, Mitchell. That's all I called to say. I simple can't take it. You know what I mean. I—"

"You'll have to come to—Jesus Christ—terms with it," Wilk groans. "Oh Lord. Oh my. I'm sorry, but this is not the —for God's sake—time for professional confidences, Jonathan."

"Please."

"I know the feeling. Please, please, faster. I felt the same way as you did in 1958, but I worked myself out of it. Worked. Worked. Worked myself. You should get an, uh, job."

"Look, if I'm really intruding—"

"Get a *job.* Job, job, job. Write short-short stories. Think of the sex market. Cultivate new friendships. Think of—" and Wilk lets out a long, dying shriek. For a time Herovit hears nothing.

"Are you there?" he says finally, running his free hand over the typewriter. "Is something wrong?" This is preposterous. He knows exactly what is going on; he should have hung up at the beginning. Still, this is perversely exciting and, in the bargain, he really does need the advice.

"Think of all your readers," Wilk says finally in a peeping, plaintive little drawl. All of his nervous energy seems to have departed. "Get your mind off the situation. Get outside of yourself. That shouldn't be too hard for a man in your position."

"Nothing seems to work. I try and try, but no matter what I do—"

"Nothing worked for me either," Wilk says slowly. "It didn't make any sense at all and it never has. There are no easy answers, but you'll get a whole new outlook when you come to academia. I'm sure you will."

"But I can't—"

"I'm sorry, old friend," Wilk says, picking up the beat a little, his words now in almost normal sequence and rhythm, "but this is really much too depressing for me. All of it. I'm not qualified to take your confessions and certainly not at this time. We'll have to discuss, I mean think, about this some other time, but not right now."

Mack Miller would not have to take this. Miller would tell this son of a bitch where to get off, would order him to shape up at once or permanently lose Survey status. Where is old Mack now? "Please," Herovit says desperately, "please, you're my last hope now. You've got to get me out of this—"

"No," Wilk says, "it's your life." He hangs up. Herovit can feel the impact through anvil and stirrups, right to the inner ear. A lot of people have been hanging up on him recently, but only Wilk has accomplished it with style; it is not a termination but a vault to yet a new level where Herovit dangles imagined legs, gasping.

Oh yes, a lot of people have been hanging up on him recently. Is this a symptom of the problem or is it one of the causative factors. He is obviously depressing people; he will have to investigate this too if he ever has the time. Add that to the list. Why not? Put it all down.

"All right," he says to the mouthpiece, "if that's really the way you want it, then the hell with you too. The hell with all of you." He replaces the phone. Screw them.

Screw Mitchell Wilk. What did Wilk ever do in his life except to turn out garbage for his part of collaborations, misappropriate funds which should have been split down the middle, and get sultry, alienated Manhattan types to go down on him? Has *Wilk* written ninety-two novels? Has *Wilk* created a whole world of magic and adventure for a generation of sci-fi buffs to sink themselves into? A review had once said that about Herovit in *Astonishment: Tales of the Recent Future,* a small, semiprofessional science-fiction magazine that had unfortunately not made it through the boom and had collapsed after only three issues. But the review was there in galleys; Herovit had seen it. If the magazine had only held out for one more issue, one more stinking issue, that review would have been printed and all the readers, five thousand of them, would have known what kind of a writer Jonathan Herovit truly was to the core.

Not Herovit. Excuse that please. Kirk Poland. Kirk is the persona, of course; only the more knowledgeable types are even aware of Herovit's existence. How did he get to this position? Even H. Smythe at Branham Books believes that it is Poland screwing the corporation, not Herovit.

"Where is that son of a bitch?" he asks pointlessly, clutching at his palms and looking at the page in the typewriter. Plow ahead. No. No more. No more tonight. He cannot even think of it. Mackenzie will have to work out some kind of special extension for him; what the hell are agents for? "Where is that bastard? I'd like to kill him. If only I could." He guesses that he is talking about Poland although, come to think of it, he might be referring to any number of other people such as Wilk.

"I'm right here, Jonathan," Kirk says. He is indeed. Rather unsteady, but nevertheless holding himself tightly erect (wavering only from the heels), tall and nifty against the closed office door, only faintly translucent against the panels, but Kirk, whose gift has always been for moves quick and subtle, could not be bothered by a factor as slight as translucence. It would never affect his style. Translucation? Maybe that was the word instead.

"I've been waiting for this for such a long time," Kirk says, "hearing you call on me. This is a terrific moment in our relationship, a real watershed, do you know that? Here I am. You didn't really call me to kill me, did you? Not that you could, old friend, but I would like to know."

Of course Herovit hasn't. What would he do with Kirk dead? Who would ever finish this novel or all the novels that must come? But neither does he want the bastard here. "Forget it," Herovit says. "It was just an impulse, just a manner of speaking, and I didn't mean a thing by it. Listen, I know I'm not going crazy or anything like that. It's just the tension and stress I'm under and this last business tonight, knowing that Wilk is getting laid. It takes a lot out of me. You can understand. I know you're not real —you're just an extension of my own weariness—but just for the moment I'll play along rather than make a scene. It's best to indulge your neuroses up to a point—I read that somewhere once when I was reading up on psychology."

"Ah, Jonathan," Kirk says in his wonderfully calm voice, balancing himself on the balls of his heels to stop the shaking and giving Herovit little knowledgeable glances and dancing motions from his fingertips, "it isn't that at all, and you know it. This is hardly a neurasthenic reaction on your part. You're *my* neurasthenia and I would have done away with you a long time ago if I wasn't such a tolerant fellow and willing to go along with things up to a point. You barely exist, my friend. You carry on at my mercy, but it's time to take some determined part in your life, that's all."

"Nonsense."

"You've pushed me away for much too long. Now you've called on me. You know you want me here, don't you?" Kirk leans forward with horrid persuasion; he has always been a rather insistent fellow—no surprise there. "Of course you do."

"No, I don't. I don't," Herovit says shakily. He seizes the scotch bottle and drains it. Tries to drain it, that is; there does not seem to be any scotch left. What could he have expected? How many has he had today anyway? Has he utterly lost control of himself, and is it true that he is an alcoholic? Forget this. "I don't want anything to do with you, and now I want you to just go away. I don't know what I had in mind by calling on you, but it was just a thing of the moment. Please. Please now, just get out of here."

"That's quite impossible. It really is. In the first place, who would support you and your wonderful little family if I truly went away? And in the second place, my friend," Poland says in a changing timbre, taking one stride forward and seizing Herovit's elbow with a hand surprisingly opaque and determined, "in the second place, I've had quite enough of your disgusting little neuroses, your rotten ambivalence, your sniveling, boring life, and I think it's time to take some real action."

This grip is hard, impenetrable. Kirk does not feel dreamlike at all. Nor close up is he yet translucent. Herovit trembles in the godlike grasp; it is a trap of culpability and now he is seized. Yes. Yes, he deserves this for having created Kirk. For having invoked his presence as a corporeal object when most writers had no attitudes toward their pen names at all and failed to take them seriously. Did Wilk worry about Dan Robinson? Did he turn into Dan Robinson to get the fucking done? (This, come to think of it, was a thought; it might bear some consideration later.) Herovit has thought about this from time to time over recent weeks—hack writer or no, he is not without introspective ability, he is a man who looks into himself— and he knows that he brought this on. No excuses. He will face the issues.

Meanwhile, the grip presses with increasing force. Kirk is really a tiger; certainly no Mack Miller, but devastating on this level—junior lightweight. Nerves and linkages in Herovit's trunk seem to go dead, and the bottle falls with a harmless *thunk,* rolling and rolling on the carpet. It stops, its neck pointing directly at Poland. *Mea maxima culpa.*

"You realize," Kirk says, squeezing, "that you're totally incapable of dealing with things any more. Anyone can see this, even your lecherous friend Wilk. Can't you?"

"Not so. It's a bad period, that's all—I've been through

them lots of times. This one is just a little worse than most. I'll be fine, really, if given a chance. I know it; I still have confidence in myself. Please," Herovit says rather hysterically. "Please stop that now. You're hurting me, I mean that." For a phantom, Kirk has a hell of a grip. Of course there is a lot of stored-up hostility at issue here.

"If I let you go," Kirk says reasonably, but opening up his hand just a trifle nevertheless, "you'll just hide your eyes and start wishing me away again, go for another bottle of scotch, and we can't have that. We can't. You can't avoid this kind of thing forever, Jonathan; sooner or later you have to face up to your basic problems and be brave."

"I'm facing."

"No, you're not. In fact, you're quite over the edge. I've watched this carefully over the last few days, and after this business tonight I've made up my mind. You're out of control, mixing everything up badly." Kirk tightens the grip to give him a resounding shake, the kind of shake which Mack Miller in his time has given a recalcitrant alien or three (how did the aliens put up with this kind of treatment? he guessed he had shorted them out), and then shoves him away. Herovit collapses to the floor, moaning, looking at cigarette ashes and small flecks of dried scotch.

"Look at you," Kirk says. "Consider your condition. Everything that Wilk said is right, although I can't say I like the man either. You've gone way downhill, you really have." Kirk rubs his hands against one another with surgical enthusiasm, walks to the window to check out the courtyard in the dark. Sometimes the superintendent and his friends lie on the stones drinking.

"Also, your life style is absolutely untenable. You can't bring up a baby in this apartment—you know that as well as I do—but with Janice's income gone you can't afford to move somewhere else, and you have no way of getting hold of the money. I'm concerned about that child, being half her father anyway. For that matter, I'm even concerned about Janice. She has a miserable life. You see those things, but there's nothing you can do about them now. It's too late."

All right. All right, it is too late. He hardly needs Kirk to tell him this; he thought that Kirk, if ever involved in discussion, would show an inventive turn of mind, but who the hell needs this? "So what do you want?" Herovit says, picking himself up and sitting weakly in his chair, averting his face. "What's your solution?"

Kirk dealt with at last is exactly as he could have known: arrogant, completely unreasonable, unable to accept those shadings of inference which more than anything else shape and control human affairs. "What do you want me to do?" No older than he, Kirk, maybe even a couple of years younger, but with the seamed and lined face of a veteran Surveyman. Kirk *looks* competent; it is a shame that he seems to offer nothing as well. "Tell me what you suggest, I'm listening to you now."

"Isn't it obvious what I'm suggesting? How explicit do I have to be?" Kirk says with an embarrassed, self-deprecatory little laugh. "I want to take over your life. Resign and hand it over to me; it isn't worth a dime right now anyway. You're completely incompetent, whereas I'm ready to go. I've got a novel to finish and a wife and daughter to take care of and all kinds of obligations to meet, and I'm willing to do this. I'm *anxious* to do it if you'll give me the chance. You might as well let me move in all the way and have a crack at this. After living off me for fifteen years," Kirk says sullenly and with a trace of self-pity, "I would think that you owe me something. I deserve a little consideration. But I need your permission. I'm a fair-minded guy, and unless you give me the go-ahead I can't take over. We'd just be two minds in the same body fighting all the time, like a couple of novels I'm thinking of, and it wouldn't be practical."

"No, it wouldn't. I won't give you permission," Herovit says, although the idea appears tempting. It would be a kind of way out. "You see, I have this college seminar to go to, and the thing is that I don't *want* to give up; I'm still interested in things. I'm just having this run of poor luck, that's all."

"Nonsense."

"I want to go to Lancastrian. It's important; it shows that I'm still valuable to someone. They didn't ask you, did they? They asked for me and Janice is married to me and the baby is my daughter." He is showing this incessant need once again to justify his existence to Poland. Strange that it should be this way; shouldn't it work the other way around? It seems there was this horror story once about a ventriloquist losing control of his dummy . . . well, maybe it was a movie he had seen, but anyway it was that kind of plot. Possibly he is just imagining this, but if there was no such story there should be, and he ought to write it himself. Although it would be unsalable if he tried. He has not had good luck at all with short stories for many years.

"I don't want to discuss this any more," Herovit says. "I heard you out and that's fair enough, but no more."

"You don't have to if you don't want to," Kirk says, peering over his shoulder at the page in the typewriter, then shrugging and moving back against the door, which seems to be his position of greatest comfort. He is accommodating; mildness has replaced the look of imminent violence on his features. Purged, relaxed Kirk. "I mean it's your life—we never argued with that part of it for a second. In fact, you know as well as I do that it's your own unconscious needs being broadcast which brought me here."

"Don't give me psychoanalytic garbage."

"It's not psychoanalytic, it's the truth! You know me, I'm not an introspective guy. Stimulus response, that's all it is. I can't do a thing anyway unless you want me to, and the fact is you badly want me to take over. Admit it. You want to give up and go away from here, put your life into competent hands, and I'm willing . . . but until you're ready to make that decision on your own, accept and not fight against it, you can't be helped. It's up to you."

Kirk the social worker. "But really, you know," Poland says, gesturing toward the typewriter and flicking his fingers, "this is pretty bad stuff and you can't go on much longer this way." He begins to progressively transluce, his voice weakening, his frame fluttering as he eases himself gaseously from Herovit's line of sight. "What do you think is going to happen if you actually get this piece of shit done and have it sent over to Branham?"

"I can't think about that."

"You'd better think of that," Kirk says. "You think they'll take it?"

"It's a contract novel."

"Stop babbling. Try thinking. You really think they're going to take that damned thing? *I* don't think they will. This is below even our quality level, and there are some things that even science-fiction editors can't take. Not many, but some. You'd better consider all of that, my friend." Poland says ominously and vanishes.

"You can't talk to me that way, you son of a bitch," Herovit says pointlessly, but then Kirk has already done so, sort of cutting off that line of argument. He wipes his eyes. Kirk's gas leaves vapors, they sting. "Get lost," he says, "stay out of my life. You do your work and I'll do mine."

No answer. Did he expect any? Kirk has always had a nifty way of closing off a scene, ending a chapter—grant him that. The bastard had experience. Herovit sighs, wondering where Kirk ever picked up a word like "ambivalence" anyway.

Damn it, if there was one way to kill a sale in this field it was to let a word like "ambivalence" slip into a final draft along with words like "subtlety" or "intimation" or "foreshadow" or "coalesce" or "tits." With a groan Herovit directs himself toward the chair; in sitting, however, he falls several levels.

He seems to have misjudged the placement of the chair, lost the damned kinesthetic sense anyway, and he seems to collapse into reservoirs of darkness, whole corridors of circumstances streaming by him grayly like Mack Miller moving into a decompression chamber to avoid the space bends, and Herovit falls and falls, already somnolent.

Dead drunk, the old bastard. Dead drunk, dead tired, wow, it has been some full day over here in Herovit's world.

15

In the reservoir he seems to recall that in the good days, when he was turning them out for Steele on the one hand and every cheap paperback firm in town on the other, five hundred on signature, five hundred on publication, in those blessed days before he had met Janice, in those fine days when he used to go drinking socially with the disbanded science-fiction guild, when he'd had a beard (before the skin eruptions started) and affected rimless glasses ... at that time he had known exactly what his limitations were and how he could solve the problems of the field. Back at that time, of course, he had assumed that the field *wanted* its problems solved.

"The only way to deal with the science-fiction problem," he used to tell various members of the guild who were far too drunk to listen (all except the nondrinkers, of course, who were busy making calculations on the activities of the drunks and how they might be put to use later), "is to get out of this field. If you follow what I'm saying.

Writing science fiction has got to be a very limiting sort of thing: most of your audience are adolescents, you understand, and most of them stick with it for only a couple years before they find out something more interesting, like how and where and why to get laid. You've got to understand that our field is something which people *outgrow,* and it's always going to be this way. So the writers have to outgrow it too, right?"

Oh my, oh my, he'd had the answers when he was twenty-four, considering things after a couple of scotches and water with the science-fiction guild. "What I intend to do," he continued, having the floor, he supposed, not that anyone really listened (no one was supposed to listen during the guild meetings; the thing to do was to get good and drunk, and at a certain point of courage you would call all the women you knew to see if anyone wanted to get laid that very second—if anyone did, you had your guild brothers beat), "is to get myself out of the whole thing in just a couple of years. I'm going to build up an excellent backlog of published work and enough royalty income so that I can take a chance, and then I'll turn out a nice straight novel or, better than that, I'll get into popular science or giving lectures to business associations on the wonders of the future. A good racket." Come to think of it—how it all comes back to him—they had *all* taken turns in the latter stages of guild meetings telling each other how they were going to get out of science fiction. Maybe the ideas he had weren't so original after all, but he was putting them together in a way which seemed original to *him;* this was one of the keystones of good writing, Steele had always said when he waxed expansive about the properties of the kind of yarns he liked to buy

Still, was it possible that he had ever really talked that way? Yes, he guessed that it was, just as he had weighed a hundred and seventy-five in those days and had honestly enjoyed writing. Face it, for all his complaining he *loved* writing because he could sell almost any kind of crap and it was found money: How long had this been going on? he still thought every time a check came through. How long will it all last? Also, in those days, he'd had little trouble getting laid for the price of a phone call or of a couple of drinks (for the new ones) maximum, usually by something that he could live with after the fact.

It was a strange thing how your life seemed to work out if you were absolutely unconscious of the moves you were making or of all the dreadful things that were lying on the side of the turnpike, just waiting to leap. Back in the old days, he had driven cars that way too: three hundred miles in a 1948 Dodge with bad steering, bald tires, and no spare in the trunk, with five dollars in his pocket, all the way from the upstate college he had attended for two years down to his parents' old home in Brooklyn, and nothing to show for it except irritation because one of the tires had gone flat just as he pulled up in front of the house. The next week the car had burst into flames and been reduced to ash, but he had not been in it; he was attending a party in a house blocks away (that was the nearest parking space he could find), which just went to show you. And he had collected more on the insurance than the Dodge had been worth.

"Trouble with the field," the guild Herovit, four or five years later, went on, "the trouble with the people in it, most of them, is that they didn't get out when the going was good so you'd have that fall-off in the standard of writing—lots of embitterment, you know, but not for me. I'll be gone before I'm thirty just like the readers are gone before they're seventeen. Has to be this way."

"You're being ridiculous, Jonathan Herovit," said V. V. Vivaldi during one of these discussions, or maybe they were merely harangues. Vivaldi was one of the senior and most drunken members of the organization, although the fact of his drinking was strange because in 1951 Vivaldi had converted to Process Religion—a sect which held that food, drink and narcotics of almost all kinds merely destroyed the brain cells—and since then had been making a nice living on the side administering the religion in one of the small institutes opened by the sect. Herovit guessed that the old man was just in it for the money, although in almost all other ways he was fanatically devout. Glasses glittering, liver-spotted fingers shaking, Vivaldi—the leading writer of the Grotesque School of the early 1940's and still fairly active in the social life of the field, though making too much money as a Processor to really do much writing—had stood to tower over the younger Herovit, quite an accomplishment since standing he was only five feet two and a half inches, although extraordinarily supple.

"Ridiculous, Jonathan Herovit," Vivaldi said again, "and if you have so little love for our field you should get out of it right now instead of exploiting it." The wonderful old man was clearly angry; like most Processors, he had a way of accumulating the poisons for months and then letting them drain in one pure surge. "Science fiction is not a form of writing, nor is it another subdivision of pulp literature. Rather, it is a way of life, a way of thinking, a new and important means of dealing with the universe. The science-fictional way of dealing with reality is the only way, and we writers have nothing in common with any other kind; *we* are a truer, finer, deeper kind of person. Someday, young man, you will realize this and be repentent of your boast," Vivaldi added, then toppling to his knees and rolling with a burble to unconsciousness on the gray carpet of the hotel lounge in which guild meetings had been held. (They were too large and unruly a group to be permitted in the bar.)

Vivaldi, it would seem, had never had the ability to handle his liquor; Process Religion had not solved the problem but indeed had made it more acute, heightened the poisonous excitation which gin exerted on the old boy's brain cells. Also passing out in the center of a guild meeting was bad form, intolerable even in this field . . . but then again, what was Herovit supposed to do about it? Was it his fault? Then again, the dean of grotesquery could hardly be left drunk and comatose on the carpeting of the lounge of the Hotel Eloquent.

Still, on the third hand (this was science fiction; you could invoke a third hand), it was not Herovit's responsibility to scrape the dean off the carpet. It was his drinking problem, he should bear his own responsibility. No one in the room, however, did anything but look at Herovit. That was the policy of the guild. They lay where they fell until the one culpable came over to assist. Usually it was the waiter, sometimes a bartender, but now and again the responsibility fell to members themselves.

"Oh, the hell with this," he said rather peevishly, settling on a compromise as a couple of the younger members, seeing that he was staying put, went over tentatively to assist the dean who was now murmuring faintly and wiping imaginary (but then again, in the Hotel Eloquent they could be real) flies off his nosepiece. Somehow he was managed back into a chair where he sat with head low, grasping his fingers and looking balefully at Herovit. "Just forget this now; you're one of the influences that we're going to have to outgrow, just like the kids outgrow us." This was not quite fair either, but then again, what had V. V. Vivaldi, now looking extremely nauseated, ever done for him? What had any of them ever done for anyone in their entire selfish lives except collect a penny or two a word on acceptance or publication, and turn out reams of misguided garbage? Well, this was not a nice way of looking at his fellow members of the guild, he supposed.

After all, they could not be blamed. It was not their fault that they were trapped, hobbyists and full-time writers alike, in this miserable little tenement of a category while he, Jonathan Herovit, far more talented and ambitious than all of them, was heading on his way up and out. He should cultivate, if he could, a largeness of spirit, a willingness to realize that his abilities were a responsibility more than a medallion, and that Vivaldi had not willed himself to be this kind of person but was in fact suffering from the consequences.

"Apologies," he murmured to the dean, whose worn face was now being wiped free of sweat in an affectionate way by the younger members as the dean lifted his old head, looked plaintively at Herovit, and then leaned all the way back, moaning. Playing it for all it was worth, the cunning, drunken old bastard. "Nothing personal, of course. Actually I've always been able to admire some of your work. Grew up with it, as a matter of fact; it set me on the right paths. You're a very significant influence in the field. Never said that you weren't." But he would be damned if he would go nearer the man than he now was. As a matter of fact, this might be his last guild meeting. A good policy. Make the declaration and get out, the saving sense of gesture. Why had he not done this? Why had he always waited for events to overtake him? Surely there was something to be learned from this.

"This man should be expelled from the guild," V. V. Vivaldi pointed out feebly from his chair. "Expelled, as has happened before in certain noted cases. He is a dilatory influence on our literature."

"Deleterious," Herovit said quickly. "Use the words right."

"Dilatory, *dilatory.* I can say anything I want because you get the meaning. This man should not be part of our guild. This man does not deserve the company of science-fiction writers."

Other members, not just the clustered young ones, nodded slowly. "You see it," Vivaldi said. "I predict a very poor future for this young man because he is basically cruel, but the rules of Processing show us that everything eventually is turned against the perpetrator, and so in the end he will become the victim of his cruelty. I remember this. I must have written it up once."

"Now wait a minute," Herovit said, standing at last. "This is ridiculous."

"No, it is not," Vivaldi said, middle-aged jowls trembling as one by one the guild members left their places to join in whispered conference about the Herovit problem. "You see, you see, young man, how they respond to me yet. They respect me."

Herovit hovered there, stunned—it was really a kind of disgrace to face expulsion from an organization like *this*—lighting cigarette after cigarette rammed through his beard, not quite sure he knew what was happening but beginning to understand one thing quite well: the guild, seemingly incapable of action, could function with expedience when it wanted. Wilk, the bastard, had been one of the participants in the conference, maybe even one of the leaders. There had been a hard core of five or six, mostly editors (he knew all the sons of bitches) who seemed to control the inner workings of the group and were talking intensely to one another; their faces glowing with the satisfaction of it all—a major expulsion! And just when the meeting had seemed so dull, the guild on the edge of dissolution from sheer boredom. And another ten or so who were neither politically involved nor friends of Vivaldi stood politely outside the conference and looked at Herovit with interest but with a lack of sympathy.

Drinking, of course. The few of the guild who weren't alcoholics at least mimed it to get along; the consumption of club soda there was fantastic.

"You shouldn't worry about this; it doesn't mean a damned thing," a fat man in this group named Francis Harkness finally muttered. God, Herovit hasn't thought of Francis in ten years; Harkness had written some satires and takeoffs for *Space Station* during its five-issue span and then had gone off to Akron, Ohio, to sell lawn mowers. "I've made one hundred and twelve dollars in a career of professional writing," he remembers Harkness as having said at another time, "and the worst thing is the feeling that I've been *overpaid.* Akron has a good library system, I understand, but I hope to never read another book as long as I live there or anywhere."

"Couldn't care less what the silly guild does," Harkness had said during this afternoon several months before his decision on behalf of lawn mowers, although even then the roots must have been there. "Don't you be concerned; you've got a great career waiting for you with open arms, and anyway, you want to get the hell out of the field, don't you? So this is a good start." Why the hell hadn't he just walked out of the Hotel Eloquent instead of waiting like a schoolboy for the verdict? Well, there was no way of coming to terms with the person you used to be, and if you ever could you'd only be in worse trouble because that would mean you had learned nothing.

At length, Wilk had detached himself from the conference and been the one to announce to Herovit that he was sorry, but they had reached a decision to bar him indefinitely, at least from the social aspects. He could come to business meetings held annually during the science-fiction conventions—that was another thing—but he would otherwise have to stay away. "It shouldn't bother you, right?" Wilk had said, very dapper then as always, checking out a fingernail and taking delicate sips from his martini, which he had brought over to help him through the discussion. "Since you say you're leaving science fiction anyway, and besides, you've really got to consider the health of the dean. He's a sick man, quite old for his years and paranoid as a coot, and you could wreck the grand old fellow by coming down on him that hard." Wilk had always been a bastard; his instincts were central.

The dean himself peeked through the shroud of bodies that covered him and gave Herovit a high, hard, almost triumphant cackle. "Going to throw you out, Johnny," the dean giggled. Herovit had always hated people who called him "Johnny" even worse than people who called him "Mack" or "Bud." "Going to teach Johnny some manners whether he wants to learn or not," and that had been that for Herovit in the guild. Permanently, as it turned out.

The suspension for insulting a senior member had been reduced to three months, not too bad considering the member or the offense, Wilk said, carrying the message out. (Wilk was always in the middle of things; whatever was going on, Wilk had special information.) But somehow, between the first month and the second, the guild, which had been on the edge of dissolution for a long time anyway, finally fell apart, wedged to pieces by the great magazine boom of the time and the consequent fact that most of the members either found work as editors or were kept busy writing by them. And the editors and writers found they hated each other even more than when they had been mostly writers.

So in the seven-year history of the guild, Herovit's had been the only expulsion. You could look it up in the fan histories or archives of the field if you were so inclined; somewhere it was all written down. It had not been nice of them to have done it (and he guessed that his friend Wilk had not argued too fervently in his behalf), but those were percentages; on a scatter-shot mathematical distribution it was bound to happen, and *someone* would be at issue. Why not Herovit, then?

Anyway, Wilk had long since made up for that, hadn't he? Hadn't he come all the way to New York just to invite Herovit in particular to attend an academic conference on science fiction and get himself laid, and wasn't all that some kind of reparation? Why be bitter? He had said that he had hated science fiction anyway; the guild had just taken him literally. There is no reason to feel shame thirteen years after the incident. He does *not* feel shame. All of this is long departed.

Well, it had been a long time ago. Thirteen years was almost five generations of readers. Still, V. V. Vivaldi, for all his deterioration, was still going on; so were most of the others, now reassembled in the larger and more business-like League for Science-Fiction Professionals. They even had bylaws now and a set of awards. Herovit had joined unhappily. He had the credentials, but had lost his taste for organizations, and then too, you could never be sure that the erratic and unstable members of the league would not get together and think of another expulsion. Fuck them.

He had certainly known all of the answers then. Oh, indeed he had. It all looked so simple then. That was the only reason to look back through all those years at what was actually a trivial incident, going to show how silly he —how silly all of them!—had been decades ago. Forget about the guild. Who knew about it? Of the five generations of readers pocketed into the field since then, would any have heard of the organization? Herovit himself has never heard of it. He will not think of it any more. It does not exist.

Perhaps it was not too sensible to go back through all of this. Science fiction was forward looking; it dealt with the future. The concern was not for vanished incidents but for the full range of possibilities for the future. It was a field which thrust out tendrils toward the rim of the possible, as John Steele liked to put it. It was contemptuous of the past except as to how it might be technologically utilized.

Well, he is sorry that all of this has come back to him. Maybe he can act as if he remembers none of it. He *does* remember none of it. That would definitely be the ticket, and it is the way things are always going to be.

He will think of it no more.

16

How can this be? This is not possible. It seems that Janice's breasts are once again filling his face, diving into his teeth, bouncing and flouncing and jouncing to and from his mouth just like in the fine times years ago before she learned words like "narcotherapy" and "aureolae" and "anesthetized" . . . and this is not possible because Janice has not had a kind word for him, let alone a true sexual impulse toward him, in months. She has said so often enough. At last he believes her. She no longer will confront him in this way . . . but when Herovit opens his eyes, feeling them unseal like 9 by 12 manila envelopes in his skull, trying to make what he can of the situation (what is happening to him that causes him to think breasts?), he finds that it is the truth. The absolute truth, by God! There she is, his own wife Janice, naked (her clothes must be somewhere), leaning over him in the bed, her face showing that blank absence and absolute determination which once came over her when she was insistent upon sex. Fed upon him as if otherwise she would die.

Oh, it has been a long, long time since she looked this way, and for an instant he can barely trust his luck—if luck is quite the word he is looking for—then he decides to ride with the situation and carry it forward as far as he can. Now that the possibility is at last his, however, he does not `.now if he is capable of acting on it. This is an old problem. He has been here before.

Lord, is he hung over. If he lifts his head for even a second, the force of it will come upon him; with old drunken cunning he does not, lets his skull loll on the pillow. His last memory is of having collapsed or something on the gray carpeting of his office, and hence toward unconsciousness and strange, twisted dreams of the old days in the guild (was he really dreaming about the guild?), but if he has actually managed to get into the bedroom where his wife is now fucking him, so much the better. No objections to that. Perhaps in her lust Janice has dragged him bodily through the kitchen and onto this bed because she could no longer contain her need for him, had to have at him instantly. Women get like that, he has read. Maybe he managed to make it through on his own. If so, good for him; he usually stays where he has fallen, but if his physical condition would allow him to get back here, it is an indication that corporeally he is not as far gone as he thought and that the daily walks to the newsstand are doing him some good.

Or then again, perhaps none of this happened or is really happening right now . . . but what the hell. Being a science-fiction writer would not be a bad life if it opened up one to the full range of possibility. Swing with it, take it whence it comes.

"All right," he murmurs pointlessly, opening his mouth wide, risking dislocation of the jaw to receive one pointing, swiveling breast as it oozes into him like paper into a typewriter, a fresh sheet to be covered with chantings of Mack Miller's courage. "All right, all right," holding the nipple between tongue and teeth, doing the necessary things to it with his old facility. Truly, you never forget. "Where's the kid?" he asks nevertheless. It is hateful of him and just kind of slipped out; maybe she did not hear. His voice can hardly be very distinct coming from this juxtaposition.

But she has heard him. "Quiet," she says. "Don't ask about that now, what's wrong with you? Are you mad?" Her eyes are closed, she looks deep within herself from this angle and seems to respond to something as if from a very great distance. It could hardly be his little organ; he barely has an erection, although he is trying. She revolves upon him, she feels that perilous enjambment, and her face goes slack. "Don't worry about it. Don't talk, don't say." She runs a hand down to his testicles and he feels pressure, further rising. Not much, but maybe sufficient. Slight engorgement, like a finger hitting a typewriter key. Then connection.

"What time is it?" he says stupidly, releasing the breast. "Is everything all right? Is it the morning? Are you well? How did I get back in here?" Surely he despises himself for these insistences, but he must ask, he cannot keep the questions down, and anyway, he is entitled to know. If he cannot take his pleasure with unsatisfied curiosity, she should be understanding. This is his house, his bedroom. His wife. Mack Miller would not feel defensive about the simple right to know. He would just plow ahead on a man's tasks. "Come on, tell me. I've got to know." Mack Miller would squeeze the information out of her as carelessly as he would sever an alien's head if it ever came to that.

"No," Janice says. "No, nothing. Don't talk now. Please don't talk." She moves up and down on him raggedly, irregularly, like a Survey Ship stumbling in orbit under the effects of an unknown gravitational pull, her lips savaging his cheeks as she rubs her face against his, laying down lazy streaks of burning like weaponry. Her breathing hits another key.

Passion. She must be seized by passion, that is the simple explanation which Herovit should accept; yet he cannot take comfort from this application of Occam's Razor. No, he is not responding as a Surveyman should; he is turned inward and querulous, the questions ratcheting around his stomach like Ping-Pong balls. Months of deprivation have taken their own penalty (and it serves her right, damn it); he is not the smoothly functioning, neatly controlled Herovit whom he remembers and regards so well. He feels himself sliding out of her, feels himself, in fact, detumescing slowly under her insistence, and thrusts himself back against her breasts with increasing force, trying to will himself into excitement, to accept the moment . . . but Janice's breasts are tubular. There are strange spots around the nipples (why did he never notice this before? they are fine and red and look as if a marking pen had pierced her with the most delicate and thorough of points), and nuzzling he feels the opposite of passion—in fact, detachment.

Why didn't she breast-feed anyway? He had wanted her

to. Any truly affectionate or responsive mother, particularly one getting along in years, would do so these days. From time to time in dentists' waiting rooms he has read articles proving that for the last fifteen years this has been a fact: breast-feeding has been making a strong return. If she had nursed the baby she might not have had those strange marks around the nipple (signs of penance, pinpoints of inference, he supposes), and why, please, is he thinking in this way? What has happened to his mind? Has he suffered irreversible brain damage in that last reeking assault upon the scotch bottle, falling at last to organic psychoses on the floor of his office last night? Here at last his wife is leaning over him, responsive and passionate, necessitous and determined, still burbling out the sounds of her seeking, trying to draw him in like a huge, soft, oddly shaped vacuum cleaner . . . and he can do nothing.

"What's wrong?" Janice says, stopping. Surely by now she has noticed. He could hardly conceal it under the circumstances and would have thought her crazier still if she had carried on. "Is something the matter with you?" She has noticed that he is not functioning in the magnificent and approved Herovit manner, is not diving into her with that swooping ease, grinding cries and rabbit-quick climax which has always been for her the sign that he is in good health and functioning normally. She groans, grunts, slaps flesh randomly over him. Then she rears up and over him, looking enormous. "I knew it," she says. "I knew it all the time. I should have known it all the time. You've gone impotent on me too, you son of a bitch. It figured. It had to be."

The baby screams from the next room. That answers one question. He twitches his head, feeling the hangover exactly where he expected, and sees the clock on the table. Seven-thirty. The day is about to begin and he cannot come. "I'm trying," he says. "You know I'm trying, but it's all a bit *sudden,* if you know what I mean, and after the night I had, well—"

"I know what kind of night you had," Janice murmurs hatefully, "and don't tell me you're trying. If you're trying and this is all you can do, then you're gone." The scream becomes hysterical. In a moment or less the child will start to kick the slats of the crib, thus conveying it in jerks across the bare floor of the dining room and eventually into a wall, where her flailing little hands might find plaster. Lead poisoning, disaster. Trying to back away from all of this, Herovit closes his eyes, feels his wife sliding away from him, hears, at last, her feet on the floor. Enough. He will deal with it later.

"This is the final straw. I knew when it happened that it would be the end and it *is* the end. I've tried and tried—"

"Tried what?" he says. "What did you try?" and then puts his face deep into the pillow, nuzzling it like a breast. Not the same thing, of course, but it might do. No room for discussion, keep his mouth shut now and at all costs don't get involved, give her no more bait. Maybe he can work it out later in the day; at least she has shown some sexual interest in him, and that could be a start. He will feel better by the afternoon and surely will be able to function then. It is unfair of her to judge his performance when hung over. "I guess you'd better get the baby," he mumbles into the pillow, purposely blurring his voice. He does not want to have to offer to do it himself, but the appearance of ordering her would be unsatisfactory too. She might, any one of these mornings, simply refuse to deal with the child, and when that happened, what would he do? Good Lord, what would he do?

"Yes," she says, having heard him, "I'll get the baby. Why shouldn't I get the baby? Why shouldn't I take care of the baby? Why shouldn't I dedicate my whole life to sitting in the kitchen and changing diapers while you lock yourself up free as a bird to get drunk and write your crap." He knows by ear, that she is lurching around the room discarding objects, pellets of clothing striking the walls almost noiselessly as she looks for her slippers . . . but he can hear every pellet. "Why don't you get the baby? What makes you so superior? One of these days I'm going to stick you with it, that's all. You think that turning out that unpublishable garbage makes you a better person than I am? I'll fix you. You'll learn!"

"You used to think I was a pretty good writer," Herovit tells the pillow quietly but intensely. "You said that what I was doing was truly important and that I had one of the most soaring imaginations in the field. Do you remember all that?" Janice's literary taste has always been lousy, however, and he does not want anyone to hear more of this, not even the pillow. That is outside the immediate problem: the overall worth of his writing, his future career.

It is enough for her, certainly. She seems to be banging her way out of the room in small convulsions and twitches, muttering curses as she moves childward. He cannot make out any of the words, which is just as well. "I'm sorry," he says into the pillow. "I'm most truly sorry," but what the hell does that do for either of them?

He tugs sheets over his head. No more testing of the hangover, no more talking, he will go back to sleep . . . but this too is no good. He cannot do it. Consciousness is a pool; he is drowning in it. Once awakened, particularly with a hangover, Herovit is awake. The pattern of the morning lies ahead of him, and it is repellent. "Please now," he tells the pillow, "spare me all of this, will you?" but he is not to be spared: the pattern of the morning appears to him as in the wicked clarity of a dream. Nauseating. He will stagger to the bathroom soon and wash his hands and face, then urinate only after much contemplation and with heavy straining of the bladder to start the precious waters. (Could this be a prostate condition? Under emotional stress he can void only with much difficulty. He is really too young for prostatitis, but then that would make it the most serious kind.) After this he will go into the kitchen, cautiously avoiding Janice and the baby, who will stare at him remorselessly, and moving to the refrigerator, will drink large quantities of orange juice straight from the container, which might cause him to vomit but then again probably will not. Somehow by that time he will be dressed—*Stop it,* he tells the cinematographer in his head. *Can't you cut this out?* but the reels grind on—and, half an hour gone, will go into his office to contemplate the novel. Fifty-one pages; one hundred and forty-nine, then, to go. This, atop the hangover, will be too much for him, and for the hell of it he will take a fresh half-pint of scotch from the cabinet in the bathroom (just a few swallows planned here and there through the morning to bring himself into focus, medicinal purposes only), and then he will start to work, ten pages an hour, thirty then by noon, no . . .

No, he cannot stand it. He is sorry he even began to think of the morning. Let's forget the whole thing, he advises himself. The charts are on the walls, but by pondering them he will force himself to live it twice, and going through it in the actuality will be bad enough. Isn't it? Wouldn't it? There have got to be limits to this kind of thing.

He sits upright, cursing. He wipes his eyes, feeling the pain working ferociously inside, shaking his head, considering the walls (portions of scattered plaster should be repainted), and delicately, fearfully, puts his feet on the floor. He stands, reeling.

Well, at least he can stand. Be grateful. Off then to the bathroom and then to the kitchen and then, at last, to the novel. No. No, he will not think of the novel. All right then.

"You see what I mean?" Kirk says. The bastard is back, fresh as morning, clear-eyed and deadly, leaning casually now against a window, arms folded. It looks as though he has been there for a long while, his posture restful and untroubled. "Just what I told you."

"Get out of here."

"I don't care to."

"You never come this early."

"You've never been so far gone," Kirk says winningly.

His attitude changes, he becomes sincere as he takes a stride toward Herovit. "Really," Kirk says, "you know you can't go on this way. It's all too dreary and depressing, and you've utterly lost any control over the situation."

"Please leave me alone."

"But now you can't even fuck. It's been building for a long time, you know; I was waiting for this."

"So why didn't you warn me?"

"You wouldn't have believed me," Kirk says sincerely. "Remember, until just a matter of weeks ago, you wouldn't even accept my existence, let alone anything I had to say. So at least we're making progress that way. But time's about gone."

"You've said that before. Don't you get tired of this after a while?"

"I do. I definitely do get tired; you wouldn't believe how much so. Now my offer still stands, Jonathan . . . but you aren't."

This is true, Herovit admits. Gasping, he sits on the edge of the bed, rubbing an ankle. He should not have tried to stand. Never battle a hangover; he thought he had learned that a long time ago. He puts his head into a palm, and feels himself dissolving.

"I'm tired of standing around watching and waiting for you to be sensible," Kirk continues cheerfully. No end to this man; he simply will not desist. If it were a matter of simple attrition Kirk would have beaten him weeks ago; it is truly miraculous he has held out this long.

"So get out of here," he says weakly. "Just be gone."

"Soon. Very soon if this is not resolved. Do you want me

to take over things or not? This is probably your last chance, you know, I've got other things on my mind too, and as I say, I've reached the end of my patience on this issue. Well, Jonathan?"

"I don't know."

Kirk gives Herovit what is almost an affectionate smile; even behind fingers Herovit cannot miss it. It is dazzling; all of the old bastard's personality and duplicity is in it. Kirk has always had a lot of personality—face it. "What do you say, friend? I told you, it's your decision."

"I'm no good at decisions."

"You've got to make a decision. You've got to take some responsibility for your life and learn how to administer it properly."

"Please lay off."

"Your trouble is that you've been dealing with galaxies and aliens and universal problems for so long that you've lost touch with the basics. Like saving your own ass instead of Mack Miller's."

"Don't be nasty."

"I'm never nasty. I'm ebullient. Come on," Kirk says, who does indeed seem dosed with self-confidence this morning, "let's go already. Let me move right in and take over. I've been doing the work for thirteen years, keeping you afloat; now you can give me a crack at the other stuff too."

"I'm so tired. You couldn't believe how tired I am. No one could. How much can a man take of this?" Mack Miller would not have to put up with this shit. Mack would storm away from Kirk now, go into the kitchen, and rape his wife over the table. But Mack did not have an infant daughter or a Doppelgänger.

"Not much more. You've got a good point," Kirk says soothingly, patting his palms in that characteristic gesture of his. For a guy with nifty moves, Kirk seems to have a fair sprinkling of nervous habits himself; he's hardly in a position to tell Herovit how to run his life. "You're beginning to look at this thing logically at last. How much longer indeed? Two months maybe, and you're in a nut hatch. Three, tops. You could go any time at all, though; you're backing pretty close in. As far as I know abnormal psychology. Of course I'm not an expert. You might last six, but I wouldn't want to be holding the book."

"But the seminar. I really have to make that engagement. I want to go and it might straighten me out, really. A few days with those coeds—"

"You're quite beyond the coeds, or didn't you notice what happened to you this morning?"

"You bastard."

"And anyway, I won't miss that appointment," Kirk says. "I'll keep it for you, go down to the seminar and fill them in on anything they want to know. Even get laid a couple of times and think of you all through it.

"Wonderful."

"You'd never make it anyway, don't you know that? Haven't you realized this, Jonathan? You'd get drunk on the train and black out before Pittsburgh. The blackouts are starting already; what happened last night was just a beginning. I watched the whole thing and it was dreadful."

"I wasn't planning on taking a train," Herovit says pointlessly. "I thought I'd rent a car and drive there; I was even looking forward to it. Or at least getting a ride with Wilk."

"You haven't driven a car in almost ten years. You'd lose control before you hit the Jersey Turnpike and go down a ravine. Anyway, even if you could drive you'd have a bottle in the glove compartment, and you'd be hitting the bottle at every rest stop there was. You wouldn't be the first man in the field to die *young*," Kirk says judiciously, "but then again, no one would have died as violently."

He comes upon Herovit, touches him gently on the shoulder. A lover's caress, faint warmth transferred. "Well," he says quietly, "what do you say to all this? It might be your last chance, right here in this bedroom, this morning. We can't go on meeting secretly any more."

"Oh all right," he says, *"all right."* As simple as that and the decision made. There it is: just like all the resolutions of all the novels. At a certain point Mack Miller seizes the objective and just barrels his way through, usually at around page one hundred and ninety. He could have done it just as easily on page eighty or thirty-three, but then he would not be writing novels; they would be novellas or short stories, and word rates and markets being what they were, how could he make a living from them? You held off the ending until the proper time and then you sprung it and another two thousand dollars was yours. What the hell did they want for their two thousand dollars: sense? Resolution? "Screw this," he murmurs as Kirk nods approvingly, thinking that he must be talking of something else. Like Mack just before a resolution Herovit lets out an even

stream of breath, purses his lips, and looks over the bedroom as if it were alien terrain. Now it is. For him it would
be. He is really leaving.

Bedclothes rumple on the floor of this planet, Janice's
dresses scatter on the bottom of the open closet, cigarette
butts are mashed here and there in the huge ashtray at
bedside. The wonderful old lamp on the ceiling above,
which has blotted out his eyesight from brightness so
many times. Goodbye, goodbye. Gloss of Manhattan pollu-
tion moving thickly against the clouded windows. Goodbye to that as well. The disheveled drawers of the bureau,
the secret little half-pint of gin under layers of socks which
he has saved for years against the ultimate emergency.
Now never to be used; Kirk's property. Goodbye gin.

"All right," he says, "I'll give up. It's all really too much
for me. I never wanted things to work out this way—you
have to believe that. I had other plans and wanted to do
truly serious work and not hurt people and change lives
and alter consciousnesses and save people from themselves, but you'd never know it from the way it all turned
out. When you come right down to it the real mistake was
in getting married. I was doing nicely until I ran into that
girl; I don't want to sound like I'm dodging responsibility
or anything at all like that, but she ruined my life."

"How little you understand."

"She ruined it. I couldn't take the pressure. I was really
very promising for a long time. Everybody said I had talent. Steele said in print that I was one of the most interesting newcomers to come into his stable in many a moon.
Surely you remember."

"Stop babbling," Kirk says dispassionately. He seems overcome by a surgical detachment, his eyes agleam with sudden assurance. Once again Herovit notices the palm-rubbing gesture, ever more measured and circular. Good God, Kirk is a maniac. How did he never see this before? Of course it is quite too late now, as they both know.

"I'm not babbling. I'm trying to make something clear here."

"No. You're babbling. I've had quite enough of your self-pity, my friend; it's never helped our situation and it plays no part now."

"It isn't self-pity. It's the truth. I didn't get myself into this; other people did. I'm not dodging responsibility, but that's a fact."

"Now you're whining. You've always had a bad self-pity problem." Kirk's eyes, gray and deep as any Surveyman's, look at Herovit bleakly. "Just a few small adjustments," he says, "and we'll be quite ready to go."

"I never wanted it to work out this way."

"It's truly disgusting to see a grown man whine and babble the way you do. You'll be much happier out of your misery."

"Now wait a minute," Herovit says, at last angered. "You don't have to insult me. You could show a little compassion, you know; this isn't easy for any of us."

"Shut up, you idiot," Kirk says kindly. "Just leave me alone right now and let me concentrate. I haven't ever done this, you know, and you could show a little compassion for *me;* here I am trying to straighten out your miserable life and all I hear is complaints." He reaches forth a hand in a boxer's gesture and grabs Herovit's shirt front. He shakes him abruptly, and although Herovit knows that he is in the hands of a figment—he still, God help him, cannot accept Kirk's reality—he feels himself falling, spinning in that grasp. The hangover overtakes him like machinery; he feels his skull pulsing.

"Come on," he says in a high, effeminate shriek. "Now just stop it, stop it!" Infuriated at Kirk's arrogance, his physical brutalization of a sick man (Kirk has a simple and cruel mind, as well he might), Herovit reaches out to tear free ... but he seems to have lost full control over his extremities. Like a man moving in gelatin, his limbs twitch and twirl disconnectedly, and then to his horror he finds himself falling. "Hey!" he says. "You never told me that it would be like this, you lying son of a bitch. You held out on me." Too late. He falls. It is very much like that business in his office last night, only much worse because now he is not drunk, merely hung over. Kirk's treachery. "Stop it!" he says. "Cut that out now!" his voice peeps helplessly like a little alien's and then he is on the floor.

The floor moves in grateful concentric spirals of warmth and need to embrace him, the floor consumes him, and Herovit sinks utterly into the panels underlying his bedroom, diving through layers and layers of space, the aspect of the bedroom now disappearing around him. The lying, hypocritical bastard. He had never told him how it would be.

But then who but a fool or John Steele would ever trust Kirk Poland? "Oh, please help me," he peeps like an alien being throttled between the strong brown hands of Mack

Miller, an alien feeling the force of Survey vengeance (he should have given more thought to the things Mack was going up against; it might have added some depth to his writing); then waves of somnolence strike him like launching sites being *bombarded* from a high place, and he is lost. Not lost. Sleeping. But trapped.

Mack looked down at the radiant glow of the insignia which had been stamped on his wrist to burn there forever, the insignia which proved that he had passed the training and was now a Surveyman First Class, one of only five in the history of the Team to attain that distinction.

The insignia meant that he was now a new man. But he did not know, regarding it, if he *felt* like a new man. He felt pretty much the same as he always had. Yet in the opinion of Headquarters he was different.

Was he truly different? Only a crisis situation would tell. Or was he the same old Mack?

The same old Mack had been good enough, he remembered, for every challenge which had faced him. He hoped the new man would be the same. He did not know. He did not know.

Kirk Poland: *Surveyman's Starship*

17

Poland speeds jauntily through the West Eighties, moving easily, reflecting meanwhile on matters of some profundity. He has been trained for years to cultivate this particular sense of balance: vigorous physical activity on the outside, calmly contemplative thoughts inside, the one giving no indication of the other. That was the only way you could survive, in this lousy world or out of it. Never let the bastards know where you stand.

Behind are Janice, the baby, the novel in the typewriter —still just fifty-one pages worth, but give him time. All in its moment; he will deal with the novel and he will deal with Janice too, come to grips with them and solve everything. (Janice is the easy one: a nasty, petulant state caused largely by sexual deprivation, but give her a couple of fucks like she used to have and we'll see her come around. Nothing serious there. As far as the baby, it looks like excessive gas—colic they called it; he will call the pediatrician later on, give the diagnosis, and get some effective medicine.) All in due course. First things first, however. Best to come to grips with his own life and circumstances, the wreckage he has inherited from Herovit.

It is good: good to be physical, to walk briskly, jauntily, through the West Eighties, heading south on Amsterdam and putting all the pieces together in his mind while enjoying the fragrant if muddled air of upper Manhattan. Better by far than staying in that drab little apartment, which in so many ways adds to the depression. Move out of there soon. Try answering some classifieds and even put a *Wanted To Rent* in the paper. Maybe Borough Park. He has heard good things about Borough Park.

Kirk inhales larger quantities of rich Manhattan air, enjoying the pollutants which, inert bodies all, seem, to revive within his lungs and start reaching enthusiastically for new territory. Good for them—in the long run they may be dangerous, but now they only provide a liveliness and a sense of disconnection which broadens his mind, to say nothing of the enlarged perspective also granted. For too long his predecessor has dwelt in narrow spaces. Now it is time to deal with life frontally. Vigor is not only for the Survey Team, it is where you find it. He will remake his life.

"Watch it, you son of a bitch," he says, as a bearded Manhattan-type taxi driver cuts a corner with ferocious speed, almost toppling him. "You want to get your teeth smacked in?" The car stops, passengerless. Oh well, it is important to deal with all problems as they arise; what destroyed Herovit was the accumulation of difficulties that could easily have been solved one by one as they emerged. Do not add to them.

The driver emerges from the cab, limping but furious. Ready for combat this one, beard or no the viciousness and limited intelligence of the New York driver seem to have been clawed into his features with a knife, and he is already bellowing at Poland as he advances upon him. "Who do you think you are anyway?" the driver shouts. "Who do you think you're talking to like that? You got problems in the head, baby. I'll belt you blind. Get away from here. Get going!"

"Forget it, son," Kirk says, holding his ground and raising his hand to the driver in a soothing, powerful gesture. "You just watch your ass now because you're in big trouble. You try anything and I'll turn you right into the hack bureau."

"What is this?" the driver says, halting, yanking off his cap and looking inside it as if for stage directions. "What kind of a guy are you? What are you talking about?"

"I said I'll turn you into the hack bureau," Kirk says reasonably. "Your cab number is right on top of the roof, you know, so everything you do is done publicly. They'll certainly seize your license." He resists an impulse to tweak the driver by his small beard; certainly he must not do this kind of thing, although it is highly tempting. It is one thing to tweak the chin of Herovit, who can be physically cowed by any gesture (*could* be cowed, he reminds himself; no more problems with Herovit), but quite another to do it to this strange driver, who might react unpredictably. Lord, though, it would be fun. "Get back in there and start driving," he says.

Kirk looks at the driver evenly and courteously, holds his ground. Truly ready for anything now, he can feel the reserve of power within him, ready to be called into action at any moment, blazing, heart-stopping, two-fisted power whose very presence the driver must sense. Kirk inhales again.

"No," the driver says, shaking his head, measuring all of this, as well he might. He is really quite young, younger yet under stress, only twenty-one or so. Probably another draft dodger like all of the new breed of taxi drivers. "I'm not going to start anything. You're crazy, man, you really are. You're hipped on the violence syndrome and you got yourself a very foul mouth too."

"Do I?" Kirk says quietly. "Well, I'll talk as I please because it suits me. That makes for a lot less trouble than driving as I please, wouldn't you say?"

Devastating, but has he been too subtle for the driver? Despite their intellectual appearance, many of them are quite stupid; beards can be a mask. But he guesses not in this case. The youth's face floods with absolute understanding, and he backs off another pace, cheeks straining.

"You are really crazy,"he says again, "but it don't make any difference to me. I mean, I can't take on the world, right? I dropped out of a psych major because I figure I don't got the right to try to solve others' problems. I got to solve my own first." He gets into the cab, lodges himself there between hanging straps and some kind of cage mechanism, and then, staring at Kirk, closes the door and moves the cab away at a grind.

Kirk stands there, watching it leave. It has been a wholly satisfying confrontation. Various passers-by, he now notes, have been standing in place and now give him looks of admiration and interest, as well they might, well they might; so few people in this borough exhibit any ability to control or direct their lives.

"Perfectly all right," Kirk says, risking a small bow. He feels good. He feels terrific. "You can do the same things you just saw me do; anybody can do them, it's only a matter of mental attitude. You understand? Just don't let yourself be intimidated; all these forces have their weak points." Mack Miller would phrase this even better, he supposes.

"Yup," he hears someone in the faces assembled say, "he's definitely crazy." Intense glances, strange winks— how had he not seen this before? They think him mad. Oh, well. He blends himself back into the pattern of the street, moving rapidly from them, hoping that they will do the same.

It is all to be expected; he will hardly take it personally. Life patterns in Manhattan are so bizarre, grotesque, what have you, that normal actions can only be taken as another strange exhibition. Of course. He has just shown them the last frontier of action—meaningful confrontation with forces inimical—and they cannot understand. Anyone out on the streets at this hour would have to be crazy themselves, he supposes—except for the free-lance writers, and even in New York there are not that many. Not to think of it. Okay? Okay. Kirk gives himself a hearty if imaginary slap on the nape of the neck and moves briskly on his way.

He will walk down five blocks and then up ten, fully restoring his circulation, and then will go back into his home, where he will begin to order his life. First things first. He will phone Wilk and demand that the honorarium be doubled; he knows how the silly bastard used to operate, and if a hundred is offered, two hundred are there, the difference going right toward Wilk's expenses. Wilk may become obscene, but Kirk knows how to handle that and remembers how Mitch would always crumple if you hit him in vulnerable areas like his chronic writer's block. And then, as soon as the baby goes off to sleep (which it eventually will; all screams must end), he will fuck the hell out of Janice. Attack her right in the bedroom, show her the new man he has become, and restore her through quick and terrible functioning. That will straighten *her* out, with plenty of time left to get to the novel. Finish it up tonight and give it to old Mack in the morning. Dig another couple hundred advance out of that old bastard too, while he is at it.

A prostitute waves at him idly from a doorway on Amsterdam Avenue between 79th and 80th Streets. With his keen vision and excellent reflexes, he notices this immediately. Blond, somewhere in her twenties, he supposes—taking it all in quickly with his extended and dependable apperception—but profoundly middle-aged behind the eyes in the way that all prostitutes, except for the very high-priced ones, are supposed to be. He waves back. Why not? Establish contact; show her that he is not oblivious of what is going on here.

"How about it?" the woman says, stopping him. She shrugs. It is a three-in-the-afternoon shrug, not a great deal of enthusiasm there, intimations of defeat in the gesture already, what with schoolchildren and old ladies with shopping bags active on the streets, and a couple of old men lying in the gutter, waiting out hangovers (Kirk has lost his) with fierce and amused expressions on their grizzled old features. Terrific old characters, probably retired seamen. New York has a multiplicity of detail to even its commonest scenes.

"How about what?" Kirk says equivocally, pausing. He looks at his watch as if verifying the time for an appointment. Never let them have the upper hand; make them talk you into it. Rates are cheaper that way. He cannot possibly be thinking of laying her now, can he?

"How about what?" she says, "How about going out?" She stands in place. The effort of leaving the doorway to accost Kirk more directly seems to overwhelm her; he can see the consideration marching through and out the corners of her eyes. Not worth the bother. Well, you had to take a lot of rebuffs in his business too; he knows how she feels. Imagine eight or nine rejection slips an hour, every hour; that would be one hundred and twenty rejection slips every working day, or forty thousand a year. He would never be able to put up with it.

"It's twenty dollars," the prostitute says after a pause, as if she were helping him price materials in an antique shop, "It has to be the twenty . . . but it can be fifteen, I suppose, if you don't want a long date. It's up to you. I don't care." Tender sensibilities. Inside, she must be suffering.

A patrol car swoops by, patrolmen gesticulating with sandwiches within as they take a right on 80th without signaling. Well, everybody on the West Side is paid off, even the pedestrians, but they could have taken a look at the old men, barely missed by their right rear tire in the turn. Then again, surely they would have stopped if actually needed; had the prostitute been menacing Kirk with a knife he has every confidence that they would have looked into the situation. Forget about the cops. "I don't know," he says, checking her out carefully the way Mack Miller would look over a new planet in the horizonator before making the decision to land (although he always did). "It's kind of hard to say." Strange to be thinking of Survey Team at this moment; that had been poor Herovit's problem, the inability to make a proper separation between his life and that garbage which he called his work. This must stop at the outset; he will purge his psychic facilities by keeping Survey in its place. Still, what would Mack Miller do if faced by an actual breathing prostitute, not an alien? It would be interesting to make that juxtaposition. Maybe if the market continues to loosen up, as he has heard rumors it is doing, he will some day be able to do a Survey novel in which Mack gets laid. *Survey Sucker.* No. No indeed. Too many science-fiction writers have become middle-aged fools by writing pornography, dealing with sex as if it had been invented purely for them at the age of forty-five, and he will not fall into that condition.

"Thinking?" the prostitute says. "Think on your time, not mine."

"I'm not thinking. I'm looking at you. What do *you* think?" A little light banter always loosened them up, he guessed.

"I never think. Gave that up two weeks ago." She risks a pose in the doorway, shows him a hint of tight breasts behind the sweater and open coat, licks her lips. She is really not that bad at all, looked at in a certain way. Maybe he had her as too young; she could be in her early thirties —those breasts promise solidity and dimension. "I just try to arrange dates with nice-looking Johnnies like you and keep the home fires burning." She says this listlessly—not too much conviction there—but they are bad lines and if she knew he was a writer, she might try harder. "Why don't you come over here anyway and let me check you out? Are you afraid of me? I don't bite, I promise. Unless," she says with a wink, "unless you ask me to. Come over."

He guesses he will. It is ridiculous to stand half the width of the sidewalk from her, conducting preliminary business with a prostitute at a distance of some fifteen feet. What he has taken for subtle, courtly gestures and maneuvers he now notices have apparently been delivered in technicolor, and a few of the old ladies with bags are looking at him. Really looking.

"The thing is, now," Kirk says, closing in on the gap and looking at her with what he hopes she will take as kindly, affectionate disinterest, "the thing is that I just don't know—"

"Oh, forget it then," she says with a sigh. Her eyes close down, her figure hardens, she draws the coat around her. Seen close on, however, she is really rather attractive. The cliché is that they look the worst when you come in close or put on more light but actually this one is not bad. She is far superior in almost all sensual details to what he has been living with for years, and absolutely better than all of his adulteries, who share small breasts and freckles. Also, he can at least suspect that once in bed she would not begin to whine and direct him to perform certain acts, comment endlessly on his abilities; this would be a new experience worth having.

"I don't know," he says again, thinking through all of this. "It's hard to say."

"I ain't going to argue with you, Johnny. You got to make your own decisions, but you started to come onto me like you wanted to go out, you got to admit that."

"Don't call me Johnny," Kirk says vaguely. "I don't like it," and then to save her feelings before she can become insulted finds himself saying, "Well, why not? Why not go out?" He would not want to hurt her; she must put up with a lot in her line of work, so to save her feelings he has made this decision.

Nevertheless, why not indeed? In one of the senses of the word he has never been laid in his life—not in *his* life, not in this persona—maybe it would be best then to practice on a prostitute. Just to make sure that he had all the moves down right. Once he has worked out the maneuvers and assured himself that he is competent, he can go back to Janice and put that situation in order as he had promised, but it might make sense to check out his mechanics first. Any sexual disaster with the prostitute will not count; with Janice it might be serious.

Then again, if he wants to look at the problem in an equally reasonable way, he has been laid literally thousands of times, most of them miserably, and hardly needs experience at this stage; what he needs is a little access . . . but complete sharing of the doomed Herovit's memories is not quite the same, of course, as having had the experiences on his own.

"Did you say twenty dollars?"

"Whatever you want. That was the price, Johnny. Excuse me—I mean, Mac." Now that the connection has been made, Kirk's purposes made manifest, she seems to possess only an abstract contempt. This might be one of the problems with prostitutes: they loathed themselves and therefore had respect for you only if you turned them down, whereas if you agreed to go with them you were obviously contemptible—but if this was so, there was no way you could win, was there? Don't even think about this. "Now, if twenty is the best you can give—"

"You said it was twenty, remember? I didn't mention what I was paying. You did. You said, it was twenty or even fifteen if—"

The prostitute is now gripped by a look of revulsion. Money, surprisingly, seems to fill her with distaste; like a paperback writer she is really quite above that sort of thing. "I won't talk about it any more," she says, "I hate to haggle. If you wanted to go more than twenty maybe we could do something. Twenty it will have to be very fast."

"But you said that *fifteen* was the fast—"

"I haven't got the time to talk here with you, Mac. Yes or no; make your move. Time is money; this is my business, like it or not."

"Yes," Kirk says, thinking now of ninety-two novels and fifty-one pages. "Yes, I guess you're right. Time is money. Money is time." The old ladies have picked up their bags and gone west, but a pair of jocular building superintendents are standing with hands on hips and nodding amiably, cheerful smiles on their open faces as Kirk follows the prostitute through the doorway. They wouldn't laugh, would they? He could hardly stand the indignity if they laughed at him. Oh well, they do laugh and he guesses that he can bear it. They are just envious, and why does Kirk Poland have to suffer under the judgment of superintendents?

Sighting his eyes as if through the horizonator on the woman's bobbing, rounded buttocks, which wink at him through her little orange skirt, he follows her up two flights of a dangerous, dingy stairway and along a hall pitted with cigarette butts and green carpeting. Different color but the same texture, isn't it, of the carpet in his own office. Although Kirk tries to keep his mind blank, he expects at almost any time to be set upon violently from behind, whole Survey Teams' worth of addicts or social decompensates leaping from alcoves to beat him within an inch of his life. And all for the simple penalty of lust! The headlines would be disgraceful, but then, stories of this sort hardly even make the *West Side News* nowadays.

Nothing happens. The building in fact seems deserted (the prostitute may be prime and only tenant), and there is nothing to fear anyway. He is Kirk Poland, no longer the target of fantasies and fears but their manipulator. This kind of thing will cease. At the end of a corridor a door opens, the woman's buttocks depart within energetically, he follows. There seem to be some religious symbols carved with penknife on the door but this is not precisely the time to stand and investigate.

Inside the room he finds that she has already undressed. Marvelously facile, but then again, time is money. Pity that Janice never learned to disrobe quickly; he would always have to *talk* her out of her clothing, and the final oozing escape of breasts from brassiere could take a quarter of an hour or longer—agonizing. This prostitute is a more understanding type; she is ready to function. She confronts him naked then, her breasts bobbing slightly, her legs spread as if to reveal to him a slightly moistened interior. He would not know about this; for all of his background, the gynecologic aspects of women are incomprehensible. Between their legs they have an orifice, or then again, it may be two, but he cannot establish which is what. Three orifices (yes, of course), but you cannot enter them from the rear in front—or then again, can you?

A trusting type, this prostitute. She has already committed her nakedness to him, although he might be a dangerous pervert or an undercover authority. He feels a surge of feeling toward her; on whatever basis, she has yielded to him and offered herself. Would that other women had done the same, without asking their questions.

"The twenty now, Mac."

"What's that?"

"I said, the twenty. You're not simple or anything like that, are you, Mac? I was afraid of that downstairs, that I'd have to break in a new one. I don't got the patience. You always pay the woman before, not after. That's a rule of this business. And I shouldn't have to ask you; you just lay it up on top of the dresser. Now you pay me the twenty now or you'll be on your way with trouble. I got time invested; I came all the way up to this hole and stripped for you, and whether you want to or not you're in for it. You want to back out, that's a problem, but you're gonna pay."

This could get quite dangerous, Kirk thinks, taking out Herovit's wallet (he will have to have all the identification changed at some time in the near future, he reminds himself) and goes through it in quick search of twenty. Stupid of him not to have checked out the wallet beforehand, and that cheap lousy bastard Herovit usually carries no more than walking-around money. It would be a real mess if he couldn't come up with twenty now, wouldn't it? He looks more frantically. Why didn't he at least peek in the wallet on the way up here? No, it was too dark. Two singles, a clumsily counterfeit five which Herovit had held onto as a souvenir from the race track for many years, and what else? What else? Oh yes, there it is. He had forgotten the escape or adultery money folded in behind the expired New Jersey driver's license; if one of his girls wanted an extra drink, Herovit had not wanted to be caught short. Well, good for him—for the first time Kirk feels a surge of feeling for the poor bastard. He'd had certain qualities.

Kirk hands a bill over to the prostitute, then examines the room absently while she does whatever prostitutes are supposed to do with their money. It is a grubby process and he will not be involved in it. The room has little enough to offer: a mattress on the floor covered with some gray sheets, a few plastic flowers in a vase on the chipped bureau, and of all things, a couple of religious portraits, which seem to have been taped to the walls.

One of them is of an idealized Savior in one of his most affectionate and winsome poses, the other of Madonna and Savior (at a much earlier age) done in pastels. Poorly done stuff this, mass-manufactured, probably available in any department store for forty-nine cents framed, but Poland feels himself oddly moved, maybe on behalf of the prostitute who needs such comfort (he can imagine her going into the store to buy these; what shyness in her hands as she picked them up to hand to the clerk), maybe on behalf of some very religious ex-tenant of this room who does not know to what use his quarters are now being put, what his hard-won symbols of belief must gaze upon. Strangeness, all of it.

"Stop dreaming, Mac," the prostitute says. She has disposed of the twenty somehow, stands before him hands on hips. "I told you that time is money; now please get your clothes off." She looks brusque, competent, but she really should stop calling him "Mac," which come to think of it is no better than "Johnny." He ought to give her some made-up name just so that he has an identity. Crude and embarrassing to be called "Mac" or "Johnny" all the time by beggars and prostitutes alike . . . but then again, didn't Mack Miller go through a period where he called all of his alien servants and runners "boys"? Yes, he seems to recall that pretty well; those were the novels of the mid-sixties. Well, Mack himself had gone a far distance since then; the aliens had become progressively more malevolent as the books had become ever harder to write, and not many of them were safe enough to be in the employ, however casual, of the leader of the Survey Team.

"Didn't I tell you to take off them damned clothes?" the woman says. "Come on." But she makes no gesture to help him. There is no contact left in this mean and brutal city, that is all.

Meditating, Kirk undresses. He exposes his slender but well-coordinated frame to the small winds and ravages of the room, feeling breezes move up and down his body, and with a sensation of utter displacement, great strangeness, closes the gap between them. Her odors assault them, mingling with the deeper scent of the room, and he inhales of her, then runs one hand across her shoulders tentatively, using the other to squeeze a mottled thigh. She breathes, breathes again, extends a drooping breast toward him and asks him to hurry.

"Yes," he says, "Yes," and finds that with her assistance they are tumbling with reasonable grace to the mattress; there he clutches her randomly, feeling himself beginning to respond. "I need it," she whispers to him, "need it, need it so badly, make it hard and make it quick." Kirk knows that this is the kind of stuff all of them pull; he should not take it seriously. She is not excited but merely wants to make time: all right, he will accept this. He is a good man, Kirk is, author of ninety-two novels and well respected for what he is, but she knows none of this and is only whimpering excitement to make him finish quickly. He is aware of this. He is no fool; he knows of whores. Writing science fiction for twenty years might not be the best preparation for life, but here and there he has picked up a little knowledge. Science fiction was a metaphor anyway; what it was really all about was whores and bestiality. Why else would Mack Miller turn his fire on the aliens without asking many questions?

Enough. He mounts her carefully, balancing rather perilously, cautious of the connection and yet eager for it. She thrusts at him beneath, doing her best to absorb him. He is hard, rigid, and that anyway, thank God, is all right. He'd had some fear, even up to this instant (why not admit it?), that he might malfunction, but everything seems to be going about as it is supposed to. Terrible if he had gone to Janice at once and found that he had the same difficulty. Mark up another good reason for having decided to try the prostitute first: he can use the assurance. In all ways then, things seem to have focused: the walk through the Eighties to increase his energy, the encounter with the taxi driver which gave him self-confidence, and now this. Sexual mastery. Life is coming into order, and in only a couple of hours Kirk has taken things further toward resolution than Herovit had done in years. Why can't he stop thinking? Why is he babbling maniacally to himself like this?

The important thing is to get inside and come; focus on matters like a true Surveyman. Enough of this. Be unthinking; just take the objective and pursue.

"Oh please, honey, you just got to wedge it in there 'cause it feels so nice and solid," the whore squeaks. "It really does." Whore talk, that is all it is and he will pay it no credence, but it is nice to know that he feels (some part of him anyway) nice and solid. Approval always helped. Had Janice, that bitch, commented favorably on a thing he ever did to her? And as far as those miserable, querulous freckled girls whom he would take to their hotel rooms at conventions—well, for all the praise they had ever given him he might have been a corpse. They saved their praise for encouraging developments in the field and their own sense of liberation. They were cautious of having their breasts touched excessively, complained of vaginal woes, complained of neurological blockage which prevented their orgasms, complained about their complexions or his thoughtlessness or the geometry of hotel beds. The hell with them. "Nice, so nice," the prostitute chants. "It's awfully nice," she sings underneath him, Kirk sings back, she sings to him, he dives mindless and sings again, they sing together in what his stricken consciousness takes to be the rhythms and diction of popular song . . . and eyes open and fixed in this extremity on the portrait of the Savior, who bestows upon him the gentlest and most understanding of smiles, Kirk convulses and comes.

He pours virtually yards and yards of seed into the prostitute, feeling them uncoiling within, whole ropes of sperm flung out from the ship of self (he must save that phrase for use some day), and he uses these ropes to clamber toward some sense of self-discovery. *Good,* he is murmuring, *good, good,* but whether it is the sex or the discovery he does not know. Call them the same thing.

The Savior winks at him; Kirk returns the wink. This is what they must mean by Grace. An understanding fellow up there on the wall. Exhausted, he falls across her, biting idly on a shoulder, and then allows his head to loll mattress-ward. Doesn't sex always leave him drained and relaxed? He would like to sleep now, if only for a short time. Perhaps the prostitute will be reasonable and let him rest, although he can understand if she forces him out. He is disconnected, utterly detached; if only he could lie here and contemplate all the facets of this life he has inherited he could solve all of them. Everything. Miss nothing at all. If only he could stay here and dream. It seems—if he could only pursue this thought in a leisurely way—that he has some wonderful plan as to how to get rid of Mackenzie, get the grand old bastard out of his life forever and yet in such a way that old Mack will think he has done it himself. He wants to think about it. Getting rid of Mackenzie. Yes, that would be a start.

The woman twitches under him, mutters. He feels the whisk of her hands grasping at air as if for a handhold; she makes plaintive sounds. Reluctant as he is, he knows he will have to release her; he does so, sliding to one side and then onto his back where with a sensation of peace imminent he lies looking at the ceiling, his eyelids fluttering. If he does not move perhaps she will stay here: work a wicked charm.

Mackenzie is his problem, he thinks . . . Mackenzie got him into writing all this crap in the first place, pushing it out harder and harder for the first 10 percent. No, this was not quite fair to the grand old man; Mackenzie had not come to *him*. And it was Herovit who had been pushing out the novels, demanding fast contracts, easy money, quick advances . . . well, no point in thinking along these lines. Just be reasonable. Accept the blame to the degree he deserves it; projecting blame on everyone at random was Herovit's device. Kirk is of a stronger nature. Still, he wishes that he had not written so many novels or had found an agent who would have tried hard to raise his advances.

"That's all right, Mac," the prostitute says. Kirk opens his eyes, sees that she is standing, already whipping on bits and pieces of her clothing with amazing facility. She is really good at this; he had no idea that a simple act like dressing or undressing could be invested with such skill. "Why don't you wake up and hit the road, huh? You'll be able to find your way downstairs, won't you?"

"Just stay with me," Kirk croaks, then clears his throat with some embarrassment. "Excuse me," he says, "I know you're busy."

"I'm always busy, I'm hitting the pavement." She gives him a distant tap on the shoulder with a heel of a shoe. "You've got three minutes, that's it. I need the room; you know you haven't rented it for the day." She goes to a closet, rummages therein, finds a monstrous handbag which must be there for the cocktail-hour trade, and moves toward the door. "You can't just lie around here,

Mac," she says. "In the first place it ain't your room unless you want to work out some kind of an arrangement, and in the second I need the space. Life goes on."

"All right," Kirk says. "I understand that." He feels clogged, stupid; the interval seems to have dropped his IQ by ten to twenty points, another old side effect of that phenomenon, sex. He moves to a seated position, crosses his hands over his knees, conceals himself. He knows that it would be ridiculous to ask more of their relationship than has already been expressed, and tries not to look discomfited. In truth, Kirk feels somewhat displaced and useless, admits this to himself, finds that the admission does not help. None of the adulteries, however querulous, had pitched out Herovit in quite this way. Maybe this is what they mean about the penalties of bought sex.

"I'll go in a second," he says. "Just kind of let me get my bearings."

"Fun's fun, Mac, but time's up and you've got to go. Be downstairs in three."

"All right."

"Don't even nod at me when you come down; just keep your eyes ahead, Mac, and walk off down the street like you belonged."

"My name's Kirk. Not Mac."

"Listen, I'm not going to get involved in your identity problems, Johnny," the prostitute says and leaves the room, giving the door the gentlest of urgent bangs. He thinks he hears her on the dark stairs but then again, quite likely he does not.

"Listen," he says, standing, wavering, "I'm a person, you

know. I write science fiction. Isn't that interesting? It should be interesting; I bet you never had a science-fiction writer before." Ridiculous—she has probably had ten if he knows anything about his field.

"Of course we're not like everyone else," he adds pointlessly, going for his clothes, "but then with your eyes closed everybody's the same. Right? Right."

What in hell is he talking about anyway? His speech sounds raving, monotonous; it does not appear to make much sense. If the truth must be conceded, it is like Herovit's. He has heard Herovit in moods like this far too often.

Maybe there is more to this mess than he thought, Kirk decides; maybe things are quite complex after all. It may not be as simple as once he had conceived before stepping into Herovit's world.

Pondering this subvocally, Kirk finishes dressing. He leaves the room, waving to the Savior, who looks at him evenly, without response. In this world or out of it, one must make one's own salvation. Stumbling down the stairs he repeats his name to himself several times—*Kirk Poland, I am Kirk Poland, my name is now Kirk Poland*—to drive the point through, but when he comes to the street he keeps quiet. Get hold of yourself, Kirk. The prostitute is off the steps, in deep conversation with the building superintendents—probably discussing his sexual functioning. All right, the hell with that. He does not nod at the woman, nor does she nod at him. Urban life is rough, contacts consequently muted. He turns north and walks quickly uptown.

The old ladies with bags are gone, the line outside the

check-cashing store on 82nd Street is lengthening and becoming meaner. Abandoned dogs squat in compromising positions on the pavement.

Evening begins.

18

At home Janice is sleeping. He supposes she is sleeping; he will not investigate. The baby in any event is lying peacefully in her crib, limbs and eyes in that waxy flexibility with which she naps. This is just as well, he decides. He would not want to try sex twice within an hour; he is not the man he used to be by any means, and he supposes he should do something about the chance of venereal infection: wash himself or take some penicillin tablets; anyway, he ought to do *something*, which he will think about later.

He is not going to see a doctor; the only penicillin tablets in the cabinet are months old, but he guesses he can wash himself and discreetly does so in his closed office over the rotted basin in the corner. The office had been listed in the classified as a *maid's room;* God help any maid who would live in quarters like these, but then again, this building dated from an earlier and more barbaric era. Some maid shipped over in steerage might find the arrangements enjoyable. There was even a bathroom off to the side, with a toilet that occasionally flushed and a shower that would produce water flecked with rust and the carcasses of a few

hapless cockroaches. He finishes his self-cleansing with an
ah, unfurls the washcloth to lay over the window sill, and
checks again to make sure the office door is securely
closed. It has a way of falling open to sudden winds, and
more than ever now he wants privacy.

Time for the typewriter. He can not delay this any
longer; he must check out the mess which Herovit has
called a novel and make a definite decision. Going to the
desk, he takes in all of it through one sweeping glance:
page fifty-one, all of the pages underneath, certain helpless scrawls and scratches which, in place of an outline, his
predecessor would use to mark up scrap paper, along with
a few dribbles of scotch. Make Mack bold, one scrawl
reads and Remember that reverse orbits have
been established and Lothar speaks re-
petitively, don't forget this to fill
out word count. Inspiring, but then Herovit had
never reckoned that these notes would be read.

Mack scratched his head and regarded
the situation with new interest, the unfin-
ished page reads. He had to make a decision
quickly now and he knew this, before the
depression struck again. It would be a
decision which would affect forever the
dealings of Earthmen with Melalbdera-
nins, and he knew that there would be no
second chance for this. That is to say,
the decision Mack made is one with which
Earth would have to live for centuries
and centuries—even, very possibly,
throughout the complete future of the

cosmos. Mack's strong, hard, steel-gray
eyes swept the horizonator as he thought
of this and then, moistening his lips
slightly, he turned and addressed the
Survey Team which were grouped anxiously
before him. He inhaled a breath of air. He
inhaled another breath. The decision was
in his hands, and the fate of humanity itself waited upon what he would say. He
knew, Mack knew, that there would be no
second chances here and it was critically
important. He took one final gasp of air,
drawing it in evenly through his tightly
muscled chest, and then he spoke. "Well,"
Mack said, "My decision on this has not
been an easy one to come by but I have now
made it. I think

And there it ends. Mack and his decision are left waiting
on perpetuity. It is a good place for it, Kirk decides. He will
leave it there.

Herovit has always had them hanging; to keep your
characters agonizing for a while was an old trick. It post-
poned coming to grips with the plot and it certainly built
up the word count. Beyond that, there was a certain purity
of phrase here to which Kirk can add nothing, a quivering
poignance to Herovit's last statement which no one could
equal. It is so rare to find Mack Miller thinking that to add
anything to this would be anticlimactic.

Quite definite; leave it where it is. Only a Jonathan
Herovit would try to slog on through a novel as obviously

hopeless as this. Kirk has had nothing to do with this one; he has not been interested in the books for years. No, he is quite beyond this nonsense; he has another and better idea.

Kirk picks up the telephone and dials decisively. He waits through three slow rings, hoping that Mack's service will not answer, then Mackenzie wearily picks up the phone and announces his full name. The silly grand old son of a bitch is too cheap to hire a secretary, probably because this would distort his image as an agent who can do everything himself. He *does* do everything himself, which is one of the prime reasons underlying his incompetence; there are others, of course. "What is it?" Mackenzie sighs. "I'm tied up in conference here."

"This is Kirk Poland. I want to talk to you about this Branham situation."

"Kirk? Kirk who? Oh, I get it. Kirk Poland, that's very funny."

"I'm not trying to be funny."

"Listen, Jonathan, I'm very busy. I told you, there's a client here and we're discussing—"

"I didn't say this was Herovit, you shithead," Kirk says crisply. "This is Kirk Poland. Get that straight from the outset; I'm taking over."

There is a slight pause. "All right," Mackenzie says mildly. "Okay, it's Kirk Poland, that's fine. Whatever you say is okay with me; I don't mind. But I'm still busy—"

"Forget it," Kirk says, closing his eyes, willing himself with this dialogue into an image of the man he always knew he could be, if given a chance. "I want to talk to you about this stinking novel you stuck me with writing, you old son of a bitch, selling it to a new market instead of to one of my stand-bys and then having them harass me." Get right to the attack; Mackenzie cannot take pressure of any sort. "I'm not going to fulfill the contract."

"What?"

"I said, I'm backing off. I'm not finishing the novel for them. As far as I'm concerned I've already met the conditions of the contract; they're breaking it by showing bad faith, trying to force me off schedule. It's blackmail."

"Jonathan," Mackenzie says feebly, "Jonathan, I think that you should watch that stuff. I warned you, I warned you what would happen if you didn't—"

"I said, it's blackmail. But I'm not going to stand for it; I work at my own speed and I'm not going to do this one for them. I cancel. You'd better get that other thousand due by tomorrow."

"Now wait a minute," Mackenzie says. He sounds genuinely unsettled, as if he had been informed that his film collection had incurred severe water damage. "I don't follow your line of reasoning. Jonathan? It is you, isn't it? This *sounds* like you, but if this is some kind of a joke—"

"I told you, this is not Herovit. This is Kirk Poland. Herovit is unfortunately no longer with us. I'm taking over this situation," Kirk says, "and there are going to be any number of changes—not that I'm getting into that now."

"I begged you, Jonathan. I said—"

"You shut up. You tell them that I cancel out of this contract and that we're suing for the grand unless they come through in a week. They can afford it. You deduct your advance to me off the top and send me the rest and then get lost."

"Please, Jonathan, control yourself. I'm an old man—"

"I'm through with you, Mack. By the time the word is spread around, everyone will be through with you. I'm going to ruin you."

"Now. Now just wait. Wait a minute there. Now wait a minute," Mackenzie says. He is gasping; in the background there are vague mumbles and curses. Someone indeed is in the office. Desperate reasonableness floods Mack's voice then. "Let's discuss this sensibly. You sound pretty upset to me, Jonathan. Like you could use a long rest. Could you use a long rest, Jonathan? I warned you about that stuff like a father, even though I'm not really old enough to be your father, although maybe I should have been. I said that it was very dangerous. Now look, there are some matters pending here, but if you'll just hold on and let me call you back in about an hour, we can discuss this." Mack has not sounded so solicitous in years. One more justification for the frontal approach.

"I don't want to talk any more," Kirk says. "Not now, not in an hour." He raises his voice to the level of threat. It is so easy to deal this way with old Mackenzie; certain people indeed are created to be beaten over the head, and why did Herovit not see this? Not to yield ground, that is all there is to it. He may even get the thousand he is demanding if H. Smythe is of the same pattern.

Allow him no openings. "This is the end," Kirk says. "There's nothing more to discuss. It's in the process of being settled. I'm out of the stable, Mack. You'll have to cheat other people; you've lost yourself a client."

"Why, you must be a crank. This is some kind of crank call, that's all it is," Mack says, his old voice cracking. He seems about to weep, and who would have believed he cared that much? "This cannot be Jonathan. This is an imposter with a vicious and distorted sense of humor and a pretty sick joke to put over on me when I've got so much on my mind and right this minute there are people in my office discussing—"

"Better get them out of the office. Whoever it is, they're just sucking around for advances; that's all you're good for. Better get them out before they take you over. But I'm not asking for any advance, Mack," he says determinedly, driving straight through. "I just want you to get that second thousand, clear off what I owe, and send the rest off to me, and then we're even. They'll pay."

"Your reasoning is terrible."

"My reasoning is very good. You tell them that we're threatening suit for nonfulfillment; they've ruined my professional reputation with these antics and rushing me on a delivery could cause irreparable harm. I'm not afraid of them any more, and I'm not afraid of you. Now get going!"

This would be an exquisite exit speech. Kirk knows that if he had the timing he is trying to learn, he would now hurl down the phone, pull the wires out of the wall and lurch from his office in search of Janice and other solutions. But he is still new at this, damn it; his sense of timing is not yet right . . . and he wants to see how Mackenzie will take all of this. Why not? There is nothing undignified about curiosity, and he is entitled to that quality. Ah, there is plenty he will learn; this is merely a break-in period. He is trying out Kirk Poland the way one would test a car. A week from now, surer of himself, he could handle this conversation even more elegantly, but he does not have a week. His life is already changing.

"It's all over," he says, listening to Mack's breath. The dedicated old bastard really seems to have some kind of an asthmatic problem; there is poor timing on the inhalation. That ought to be looked over by a specialist. He thinks of giving that advice, then decides not to bother. One thing at a time. "All over," he says again.

"I don't understand this." Mack's voice has aged; now it quavers. Kirk has a vivid image of how it must be over at Mack's place about now. Mack's face is bloating, expanding with senility like that of an alien when exposed to the Survey evacuation chute. Wrinkles are popping out like weeds all over his cheeks and he has become eighty years old; yet the begging client in his office will ignore the evidence, still hoping that he can grab the money. "This has *got* to be some kind of crank call. You'd better cut this out, Jonathan. You've been spoiling for a long rest for years. I wanted to tell you that, a lot of people in the field have noticed this and have asked me from time to time whether I'm trying to help you, but I've been protecting you for a time. We'll have to discuss this, Jonathan. That is, if you *are* Jonathan. If you aren't and are just taking advantage of a very sick, damaged writer, then I want no part of you either." Mack terminates.

Oh well, he was bound to do it sooner or later; this is probably as propitious a time as any, although it is humiliating to have a phone clatter on you. Musing, Kirk sits looking at his hands, curling and considering them, meditating and counting off the seconds. In twenty-five it rings.

He picks it up quietly and holds the mouthpiece against his lips, as gentle as a beloved's hand. "Jonathan?" Mack says. "Jonathan, is that you there, finally? Now, the strangest damned thing—"

"Get me the money," Kirk says, "or I'll have you thrown out of the agency business." He puts the phone down firmly and works off a slower twenty-five. No ring back. Good. The message has been delivered.

"Ah, well," Kirk says at last when it is apparent that this time Mack will not call again. For an instant a wisp of boredom—or is it panic?—touches him; now that he has dealt with that problem he must move on to others, must continue to order and arrange his life . . . and yet it is so difficult to do so; he will admit to himself (none of Herovit's lies now—Kirk is an honest man) that he wishes Mack had, well, made it a little *harder* for him, showed just a shade more reluctance at allowing Kirk's stand. It is so pitifully easy to disengage from one's life, Kirk now begins to see. One thinks that one is hopelessly enmeshed in people, situations, deadlines, necessities . . . and it appears that with no more than a few gestures—five or six at the most —one can get away from all of it.

It is not a pleasant thought, but then again, he might as well confront this: the *ease* with which most of his entanglements will allow him to slide out of their lives is unsettling. He thought that he had mattered more.

"Ah well, ah well," he repeats, his voice sounding a little shrill in his ears, and then he stands, uncurls his limbs (a little stiffened from the activities of the day so far, but still not bad, not bad at all; Kirk is sure that he has a certain leonine grace which if he were vain enough to look in a mirror he would surely find), and leaning over, takes the first fifty-one pages of the final Survey novel from the manuscript box in which they have been lying (does he really think this?) with an apprehensive and pleading expression. He holds them, slightly warm to his hands. These pages seem to radiate sullenness, and he looks at them for a while, considering the prose style, looking over the last Survey. "I think," Mack had said, and Kirk guesses that this is the key; Mack is *thinking* and this has never been Mack's strong point; once he started to cogitate he was in more trouble than he knew and had perhaps lapsed beyond understanding.

"Fuck you, Mack," Kirk says quietly. "Get lost, baby."

Very determinedly, he tears the pages in half. One hundred and two of them now.

He fondles the one hundred and two halves, then makes quarters of them. A little more effort this time. Two hundred and four quarters which he stacks neatly, although the edges, as could be expected, are now beginning to protrude, and it is not as easy to assemble them as it was fifty-one or even a hundred and two. Four hundred and eight? Can he do it? Does he have the strength?

He guesses so. Groaning, he creates four hundred and

eight little pieces of the last Survey, a few of them sifting idly to the floor like cow dung dropping to a barn floor. A barn—that is what this office has always reminded him of; now he can make the equations as never before. The fetid odor, the little window admitting only darkness, the oozing heat from the radiators, the bovine murmurings and mooings from the courtyard below, his own moans and little cries of pleasure as his udders are stroked, unsterilized little words splashing to paper. Flies murmuring in the summer, darting around his ears; the lusty cries and clatter of cans below as farmhands or garbage men feed their trucks. Another way of looking at the life style. Of course it does not change it.

Yes, he has the strength. "Fuck you, Mack, fuck the Survey, and goodbye to you all," Kirk says affectionately but noncommittally, like an attendant beating a mental patient. He winds up like Koufax in his prime (another fantasy, well discarded by this time) and hurls the pages at the wall.

What he wants is something sensational, of course: fire, dust, heat, explosion, exit fire. But dull to the end, the free-lancer's life can yield little drama. Paper, even clumped in a mass of four hundred pieces, is virtually weightless. The clump hits the wall quietly and with an anticlimactic whisk drops in a large mass to the floor, only a few vagrant sheets bothering to segregate themselves and managing to crawl, semi-anthropomorphically, across the floor. For all of his effort, he has merely given himself another cleaning job.

Looking at this through glazed, distracted eyes, Kirk

sees the paper scatterings as little Mack Millers. There they are, several hundred of them, reduced to shrunken eighth-sized proportions, desperately trying to escape the deadly destruction of the last Survey. They wave their little hands at him, scrabble their limbs, make pleading gestures.

"Can't do, Mack," he says warmly enough. "It's impossible for you to make it," but Mack still tries. Conditioned by ninety-two novels of struggle and adventure, the tiny bodies struggle through layers of exhaustion and pain to escape certain death. "It hurts, it hurts," five or six of the Macks (the largest, the spokesmen) peep in wee voices, collapsing on the floor in droves, the cataclysm overtaking them as Mack, the fool, should have known would happen. Did he think he was immortal? But he will die fighting. "Stop it, stop this please," they peep but too late. Kirk watches them intently, the referee. It is quite hopeless. They rest in place.

They are dead.

"I'm sorry, Mack," Kirk whispers, rubbing his palms. "Truly sorry, but it had to be, don't you understand that? It's for your own good." His voice lacks conviction; he is more moved than he could say. "For your own good—you were suffering terribly, you know, and nothing would have come of this.

"Nothing would have come of it; you've outlived your time, Mack," Kirk says, trying to drive the point home but still no response. The Millers are speechless; from best to least of them they have nothing to say and cannot—is this what he wanted?—grant absolution.

Quietly, Kirk lights a match from the box of kitchen matches on the window ledge. He kneels, sets the little pieces one by one to flame. The stench is terrific, blinding and nauseating him, but he continues; Mack would have wanted cremation. Hadn't he said that once? When the time comes, I want to become ash and part of the great deeps of space. Yes, he remembers writing that, somewhere, a long time ago. All of the novels jumble together. Perils of commercial writing.

The Millers are now ash. Ash and sediment, all of them, except for one which is left, decomposed. Carefully, lovingly, Kirk stamps all but this survivor into the rug, spreading out the ashes with a toe. He is suffocating in the odors of burial, but will not stop until they are scattered. Dying, the last Mack faces Kirk with curiously blank eyes undamaged in his face and says, "This is pointless, you know."

"No, it isn't."

"You're not accomplishing anything and you haven't changed. Any of it." His edges curl, little wisps of smoke assault this last Mack. Fighting to the end he struggles . . . but Kirk strikes one, last tentative match and now it is done. Gray little stains on the carpet, the fading of silvery voices. Agony in the corridors, and now darkness.

Done.

Kirk stands unsteadily and tosses the matchbook into the wastebasket. Coughing, he staggers to the desk, takes one small drink of scotch. He had meant to be an abstainer, but so much, so much for intentions: he deserves a drink. The scotch implodes within him like a fireball. He feels the nuclear cloud growing in his stomach, the gentle

radiation soothing him, causing him to expand in subtle
ways.

"You should have done it years ago, you stupid son of a
bitch," Kirk says. "I blame everything on you; it's your
own fault," talking, he supposes, to Herovit, and he must
not allow himself to do much of this; what is Herovit to him
or he to Herovit? He leaves the office, opening and closing
the door quickly against the stench lest it fill the apartment, and prowls toward the bedroom.

And Mack, reconstituted, rises transmogrified and terrific against the screen of consciousness, points a finger
now huge with accusation and grief. "Pointless!" Mack
screams. "Pointless, pointless, stupid, stupid, waste, waste,
waste!" Before Kirk can get at him, he drops clear away
through the trap door of retrospection as Kirk, filled with
rage that he is only beginning to understand, lunges toward the bedroom in search of his and that damned Herovit's wife.

19

His idea, he supposes, was to mount her roaring and to
so transport her past resistance, past insistence, past questioning and doubt to some level of physical sensation she
had never before suspected existed. Like in a sex novel, it
was amazing how being with a prostitute could open you

up emotionally, change your way of looking at many things. But when he charges into the bedroom, determined and confident, ready to show her this new Kirk, new husband, he finds that the situation has changed, and that his seed and attitude mean nothing.

The Janice he recalls from the morning is not the Janice of present time. There she is in the bedroom, but not resting: refreshed, alert, she is surrounded by bags and bags, stray suitcases which she seems to have taken from every closet or stolen from the street, some of them spilling out clothing, some yawning through their hinges. Gasping, she folds her arms, glares at the cases and then at him.

"What is this?"

"I was afraid you'd be in eventually. I knew it; I've never had any luck. If I had only a few more minutes though."

"What's going on?" Kirk says, although he knows all too well what is going on. It is like a scene he might have written—quite badly—any number of years ago, although he cannot reckon with the factor of surprise. Strange—immediacy will unsettle us all. Natalie, almost hidden behind rumpled clothing on the bed, seems to give him an indolent wave. He waves back. Why not? Strictly speaking, he is her father. In the biological sense anyway. "I want to know what you're doing," he says pointlessly.

"What does it look like I'm doing? Have you gotten that stupid?"

Nettled, Kirk says, "It looks like you're packing up to leave"—of course—"but you're doing one hell of a disorganized job, and you might be unpacking for all I know, having changed your mind. In any case, there's no need for this, Janice. Quite a few things have changed and I was just coming in to talk to you about them. I think you'll find that if we can sit down reasonably and have a talk, you'll be very pleased—"

"We haven't had a talk since I told you I was pregnant."

"Whose fault is that?"

"You said it was wonderful that I was pregnant and I'd better quit my job as quickly as possible to preserve the health of the baby. You actually said that! And that was the last time we talked about anything."

"Did I actually want the child?" Kirk asks. "I really said that?"

"Oh, leave me alone. I'm going to move into some kind of communal type of arrangement, if you want to know. I've checked out some possibilities, and there are quite a few extended-family situations in Brooklyn that look worthwhile. But that's all you're going to hear from me direct."

"Oh, come on, Janice," Kirk says reasonably, kicking at a suitcase. "This is ridiculous. Extended families. Brooklyn!"

"Of course I'm going to have the lawyers get you for everything you have, but that they can do themselves. I'll let them worry about it; if they can get you for half your income, what would I get anyway? Two thousand dollars?" Distracted, she pulls down her sweater, displaying her breasts prominently. Really, he has not seen Janice so animated in years. Her eyes reflect light, her head bobs; her breasts are not only full but look uptilted from this angle as she leans now to take sheets randomly from the pile of them on the bed. "I'm going to straighten my life out now," she says, still inexhaustibly talking, but there is a modulation and an enthusiasm which Kirk has never heard. Desertion seems to favor Janice. "Problems are problems only if you don't face up to them, but I admit it. I admit it now, baby," Janice says grunting, squeezing the bedclothes into a smaller shape and heaving them enthusiastically into a bulging suitcase. Well, she had never been much of a housekeeper. "I admit that I have a problem, and by God, this time around I am going to solve it."

The baby giggles. "I ought to dump the kid on you," she says, her head moving convulsively. "Believe me, I gave it a lot of thought, this stupid tradition of the wife taking the children, and who needs it? For that matter, it's the husband who's supposed to clear out in these things, not the wife at all, but I'd never get you out of the house, so what's the difference? If I left her here you'd probably abandon her anyway." She is chattering away as she has not since the day he met her; she was twenty-four years old and wanted his autograph. "Unless you say you want her, of course. You can have permanent custody; I'll sign all the papers. But no such luck."

Truly, not since the Honor John Steele Society or at least since the middle of their courtship has he seen Janice so filled with life. Divorce and alimony, abandonment and flight, destruction and darkness, seem to have given her, like Mack Miller, all the energy he thought she had lost. "Well," she says after a pause, "*do* you want custody? I'm getting out of here in just a couple of minutes. I almost made it clear out without having to talk with you, but no such luck. Well, maybe I can *make* luck out of it. Tell me you want her."

"Now, let's just wait a moment," Kirk says. It is so much easier to reduce the pace of a scene in the novels (write a long description of the interior of a spacecraft, say, or discuss for the hundredth time the expressions in Mack's eyes and how they got that way) than it is here, where events seem to overtake. Herovit has had his problems in this household, Kirk can see that. Easier, maybe, to write novels and give advice, not that this is the time to consider any of that. He sits on the bed, lifting the baby like a giant fork to push her over slightly; he does not want to sit on her tines, or legs. "Let's discuss this calmly, if we may. I don't think that you're giving me a chance. The situation, as I say, has changed somewhat and—"

"Nothing's changed."

"It's changed a great *deal* and if I can fill you in you'll understand." How can he show her that he is a new man? The bitch does not listen; this is her fault. Never has she listened to anyone. Mack Miller would not have to put up with this shit.

"Nothing's happened, nothing's ever going to happen. I thought that through and I accept that. You'll never change, just go on this way for years and years, and wind up someday like that disgusting Mitchell Wilk. That I knew. But when you turn up impotent on me this morning, that's like the end. I'm going to take the clock on the table and the television set; you don't need that stuff and I'm entitled."

"Turned up impotent? Did you ever do anything to encourage me, to—"

"Not going to talk any more. I called the movers and everything; they ought to be here in just a few minutes." She stretches he sweater again, stands. "It's one of those fast firms that advertises in the neighborhood—move you anywhere on an hour's notice. I know just what to do, I think. What's changed, Jonathan?" she says distractedly, sitting on a suitcase to close it, her fingers curling away suggestively at the vinyl as she does this. But she had never liked to touch his genitals. "Did you finish another chapter? The whole novel, maybe? Did you figure out another way that you can cheat that old bastard Mackenzie out of some money? Or maybe you sold Norwegian rights to something for twenty dollars."

"No."

"God, how I hate science fiction. I hate everything about it. I hate the people who write it and the people who edit it, and don't forget the idiots who read it. And the word rates and the conventions and what people say to you if you're married to someone who writes this crap."

"It's an honorable field. It foretold the splitting of the atom and the moon landing."

"Like hell it did. It was just a lot of crap, all of it, and a couple of lucky guesses."

"I can't argue the field with you, Janice," Kirk says. "You used to like it."

"Like what? How can you all take yourselves so seriously? You really believe this garbage. You write about the problems of the universe and alien invasions and space flight and worlds being blown up and the fate of the galaxy, and you can't even straighten out your own lives or make more than a penny a word. All you do on your own time is complain about the lousy pay and the lousy editors and get drunk at those conventions. I think you're all insane," Janice says with some conviction. "I've had a lot of time to think this out over the last few months, and I mean it. There's a craziness in the field; it's just right into the middle. Once you start writing the stuff you're out of your head already."

"You didn't think that way once."

"But I never took it seriously! I never even liked it! The only reason I got involved with it twenty years ago was because even though I was not good-looking, there were so few girls of any kind hanging around science-fiction clubs that I found I could get all the dates I wanted, even if I was going out mostly with losers. See, I can admit it; I can face the truth and say it out loud but you can't. You see," she shouts, hurling a miscellaneous assortment of nipples, bottles, streaked diapers and Vaseline jars into another suitcase while Natalie pivots to her stomach, watching courteously, "I *can* face the truth, but you can't. I outgrew you a long time ago, probably before we even got married. Married," she says and shudders, "now there was the stupidest thing of all, but there's no point in looking back at the past, is there?"

Her breasts are excellent. Call it deception of cover; he cannot recall them as having been *this* promising, but nevertheless Kirk wants to touch them. Unusually large breasts, if slightly pendant and with those strange markings around the nipples . . . how long since she was truly taken with desire? That would have solved everything. If only somehow he could break through and give her the fuck of her life . . . but she catches this as if it were written across his forehead, flicks an elbow across her chest in concealment, and closes this latest suitcase. "Don't even think of it," she says.

"Why not?"

"I couldn't even think of having sex with you. I may never be ready for sex *again,* although I can hope, can't I? Maybe I'll even be able to enjoy it some day, but I'll probably be forty-five years old before I know what it's like to come." Cruel, cruel. His feelings are protected since he is not Herovit, but nevertheless it is a vicious stroke. In fact, he could kill her for this. In fact—

The buzzer lets out a moist burst of static, much like a yelp. "That's them," she says gratefully. "That's the movers. I warn you, you say one *word* to them or try and stop me in any way and I'll do something—well, I'll do something drastic." She does not like this anticlimax, he can see. She shakes her head as if at her own failure of rhetoric; he knows the feeling. "I mean it," she says and leaves the room.

Kirk leans on his elbows, hovers over Natalie, inspects the baby. In the fat little cheeks, the cast of her eyes, he can see some resemblance to Janice and maybe to himself, but it is nothing spectacular. He would like to be moved but cannot. Fathers were supposed to have strange, complex feelings when they looked at their infant children—weren't they?—but he has never had them.

Staring at the child, who lies blank under his gaze, Kirk can now see Herovit's problem, feel a tug of that depression which undercut his predecessor. The child, at least seen in this way, is so utterly without charm. She is so corporeal, so *self-assured* in her helplessness. "Aren't you?" he asks. "Isn't that right?" Natalie gives one gurgle, fixes her eyes (slightly crossed) back on him, and then begins to scream.

Well, he cannot stand it. He backs away quickly, the child's sounds fading. It is not fair to feel this or to think it, but having looked at the baby in this way, Kirk can even sense a tug of *loathing.* Unfair, of course. The child hardly asked to be brought into this world.

But neither did Herovit or his wife. Kirk had, but that was of a different order. Most people did not want to be born into this world, and on that basis then, he can hardly excuse the child from culpability. She is responsible for her existence, as responsible as any. She must pay the penalty.

"What penalty?" he asks the baby. "Well, I'll think about it and let you know. Anyway, I want you to realize that I'm not blaming myself for this, and you can't. I am not responsible. I was not the agent of your birth—except biologically speaking, and even that could be argued." Natalie screams again, carefully. It all seems a little beyond her comprehension, as well it might be, although she kicks her little legs willingly enough and fixates her gaze upon him.

"Oh, just forget it," Kirk says. "Forget the whole thing. I'm sorry I brought it up. He could take custody of the child—certainly he could, who would stop him?—but no, it wouldn't work out. Herovit might be able to do it, being so conditioned by defeat as to take on this kind of life, but it is hardly for Kirk. Kirk is active; he is functioning; he could hardly get things in order if he had the constant obligation of baby care.

Then again, this might have been Janice's problem too, but he will not think of this. Give her no sentiment or understanding; what has she given him? Nothing, not even the chance to explain, and if she will detach herself from him he must do the same to her. "I said forget it, damn it!" he shouts. The child laughs at him. He risks a tentative gesture and finds, as he should have suspected, that Natalie has wet her diaper.

The hell with it. It is Janice's life, Janice's problem, Janice's baby—let her take care of the situation. One way or the other she always has, hasn't she? "I've had enough of this," Kirk mumbles. "Mack Miller wouldn't have to put up with this shit." But Mack was not only a virgin, but childless.

Janice enters, followed by three marginally depressed young men with mustaches. They look like poets or guitar players, but then that is the style nowadays; the cabdriver had looked like an aesthete himself. "Take those," she says, gesturing at the suitcases. "Take everything in the room that doesn't move except him, and I'll take this," and she picks up the baby, making a sour expression as she notes the wetness.

"Leaving your husband, lady?" one of them asks.

"Something like that."

"Very common these days. Most of our rush cases turn out to be something like that. Don't worry; it'll probably be the best move you ever made. A far, far better thing and so on."

"Don't be too sure of anything," Kirk says. "Just don't step in and start to analyze situations, huh?" He is at a disadvantage and disconcerted, to be sure, but he will not give them the satisfaction of leaving the room. He will not. He will hold his ground. This is his apartment.

"Don't get nasty," another mover says. They not only look but talk the same: high, uninflected voices suitable, Kirk supposes, for folk ballads. "It's probably your best move too, for sure. Any time you come to the point of a split, you got to go ahead and make it. I've been through this myself." He hoists a suitcase, lifts another, struggles from the room.

"I don't want the furniture," Janice calls to him. "That's staying."

"The others are the furniture men; you talk to them."

"All right," another mover says, "you talked to us already. Just suitcases, okay." He takes a pair, the other does as well, and they leave grunting. Natalie squeals, Janice hikes her up.

"You know," he says, "you're really being impulsive about this. If you'd only give me a chance to discuss—"

"No. Never again. I wouldn't ask you for your name."

"Let me tell you my name," Kirk says earnestly. "That could be a start, because you see everything has kind of turned around recently—"

"Don't you understand? I don't ever want to speak to you again once I leave this apartment. If I ever *do* speak with you or even hear your name mentioned I know that

I'll be traveling in the wrong circles and I'll bail out. Who would know your name? The only people who would know your name would be the kind I look forward to spending the rest of my life away from. And that's definite," Janice says. "That is very definite." Nevertheless, she does not leave the room. There is an expectant look on her face. Obviously she wants to be cued for a more effective exit line.

"Are you sure?"

"Oh, I am sure. I've never been so sure of anything in my life."

"Then go," Kirk says. The hell with it. The scene is becoming circular.

"I am," Janice says, somewhat disappointed. He can tell. "I very definitely am." She leaves the room then, dangling the child from the crook of an elbow. Natalie seems to be making a tentative bye-bye, but Kirk would not like to be unduly sentimental. Not any more.

The movers reappear as Janice leaves, whispering to one another about the lastest opening in the Yale Series for Younger Poets contest, and get the remainder of the suitcases, waving at him. Simple, so simple: two loads of suitcases for three movers and she is out of the apartment. How little there must have been to the marriage if five minutes of work will take out everything she feels she needs from it. Still, it is not really his fault.

He follows them awkwardly to the door, peeping into the dining area where they are now loading all of the cases on a large, rubberized dolly. A pedantic urge overcomes Kirk. "This really wasn't necessary, you know," he says, feeling somewhat like a television commentator. "If you only knew the real factors here you'd see—"

"It's for the best," a mover says. "You get into this line of work, you find one of these situations a week, and it shouldn't bother you. Just statistics, you know? Don't feel you have to apologize or justify; there's nothing to explicitly rationalize, and besides, the quicker we can work the quicker we'll have the lady out and start you on the way to feeling better."

"She doesn't even know why she's leaving! If she'd only admit—"

"They never know. But they think they know, which is just as good as the real thing—at least that's my theory. Am I right?" The other movers say that this is probably right, although one of them has qualifications.

"They're deeper than we are," he says, putting up the last suitcase, "and I don't think that you can really analyze these situations." The dolly is trundled to the door and then, with a few maneuvers, out of it. Kirk follows them into the hall. Damn it, he deserves to get his point across.

"I have rights," he says, "which are being violated here. If only someone would let me explain—"

"Why?" one of them says. Pity that they are indistinguishable; if Kirk were writing a novel he would have a hell of a time dealing with a set of identical characters. You have to do *something* to individuate—otherwise the scenes drag, become muddled and jumbled—but what can he do here? A stutter, a limp, some hint of effeminacy whisked into place to define the movers would certainly be necessary, but life (Kirk agrees, standing and looking at this) does not duplicate art and is not even on speaking terms with it, and the movers, sad to say, interchange. "What does it matter what we think of you?" the mover says. "All we are is like minor characters in the five-act play of your life. We walk on and then return backstage, we got almost no lines or involvement, and besides, we'll never be back again. If this were a play we wouldn't even be there for the curtain calls. What do you think we are?"

"I don't know."

"It doesn't matter. Man, you have got the wrong attitude about this thing if you think that we have anything to do with you at all. No one has anything to do with you; this is your life and you'd better have a look at your priorities."

The elevator door swings open with a thick wheeze. "See what I mean?" the mover says somewhat obscurely, looking inside. "This whole thing is metaphysical. It isn't on the reality plane of things at all."

They push the dolly into the elevator. Unfortunately, there is no functioning service elevator in Kirk's building, and a fat woman, trapped now in the back by the dolly which rolls ominously right up to her stomach, gives Kirk a look of rage. He thinks he might recognize her as a dog-feces protestor from a recent tenants' meeting, but then again he may have never seen her before. Most fat women look alike, and after all, relationships in this city of alienation are so fragmentary that there is no contact. "You bastard," she mutters to Kirk. He can hear this distinctly.

He shrugs. "Not my fault," he says. "It was my wife's. Talk to her."

This seems to make little impression upon the passenger. Her mouth works subtly; she seems to be mouthing out curses.

"See what I mean?" the metaphysical mover says with a wink. "That's another part of it. It's just a situation that can't be resolved by, like, the more conventional means. Isn't that right, lady?"

"Drop dead," the woman says, and the mover makes some remark about J. D. Salinger as the door whisks closed. The elevator falls. With some timing it might at last decide to give leave to its supports and fall to the basement, but then again it probably will not; this is fated only when Kirk is in it. Even if it did collapse, though, this could hardly be construed as luck. The passenger would sue for enormous damages on the basis that it was Kirk's movers and the weight of his possessions which caused the elevator to lose cabling, and she would probably win the suit. In criminal court. He always had suspected somehow that he would die impaled on a fat woman. For that reason all of his adulteries had been thin.

Now with an overcoat, Janice comes out of the open apartment carrying the baby. It is her dress coat thrown loosely over her shoulders; underneath that she has changed to a white sweater which does as well for her breasts as what she had on before. Small threads of perfume seem to drift from her and a hint of cosmetic delicate on the upper cheekbones. Really, she has not looked so well in years. Flight, collapse, disaster, desertion have made her gay, as all of his blandishments have not. She presses the call button and stands at peace, silent, waiting. Natalie reaches over a shoulder and caresses his cheek.

Well, at least the baby cares. Doesn't she? Too young to have been taught hatred, she can reach trustingly for Kirk. Then he feels the little nails digging in and wonders. "Cut it out, goddamn you," he says, backing away. The baby smiles. So much for sentiment.

"You might as well talk to me," he says to Janice after a time. "This is ridiculous, walking out on a man without even giving him a chance to explain. I've tried to tell you—"

"That's what I'm afraid of," she says, "your telling me." The elevator comes back, the door opens; the car is now empty. "Your telling me things," she says. "Do you know something, Jonathan?" she says, entering gracefully and pivoting to look at him for her last shot. "You are a very dangerous man. You could be a killer." She waits for the elevator door to close but cunningly he has put his finger on the button, a secret trick known only to certain tenants as a way of tying up service. "You could be a killer," Janice says more doubtfully and then sees what he is doing. "Let that go," she says. "Now, damn you, just let it go."

"Explain what you mean," Kirk says. "Come on, finish it. What are you saying?"

"Let it go!" Furious, Janice has lost her timing. Like old Mackenzie she is not at her best under pressure. "I'm through with you. I've said all I'm going to say. Now you let that door go or—"

"Or what?"

"Please. Please let it go." Yes, indeed, how quickly she can be reduced.

"You're starting to plead now. You go very quickly from accusation to beggary, don't you? Have you thought about this problem?" Kirk feels the meanness percolating within, small bubbles of revulsion as invigorating as anything today, even the sex. His cells liquefy in those bubbles, begin to flow. "Have you?"

"Let it go or I'll take the stairs."

"No, you won't," he says, extending his free arm to demonstrate that she is trapped. "That's a bad idea entirely."

"Then I'll throw the baby at you," she says, her face losing its fine lines and becoming blurred, amorphous, more like the Janice he has known. "I swear to God I will." She holds up Natalie; the child looks at him impassively. "Then I'll tell the police that it was all your fault. I don't care. I don't care what happens, I've got to get away from you so badly." She cries. "I don't care for you any more. Can't you see that? How long must this go on? Won't you let me alone?"

"All right," Kirk says, "I hear you now." He steps back a pace and slowly lets go of the button. Like feeding the first page of a novel into the typewriter: the same trepidation, the same loss. The door slides closed. In the emergent dark porthole he can see his wife's face, tiny, trapped in cameo as the elevator collapses downward. An archaic look to her—she might be hung and dead. He looks at the cameo for an instant; then it falls from him as if held to the wall by cheap, frail glue.

The elevator makes its sounds as it works its way down.

He presses his shoulder blades into the plaster of the wall opposite, listening. Disconnection oozes through him; Kirk wonders what he is doing here. He should not have come, should have left it to Herovit then; it is his wife, his problem. Ironic that Janice left him before giving him a chance to talk (but would his explanation have helped at all—she would merely have thought him insane), and inevitable.

Not easy. None of this is easy. How could he have thought it would be? Herovit had had almost twenty years to louse it up; how could Kirk come in and pick up the pieces?

"No way," he says. "No way. The hell with it." He walks through the open door of the empty apartment and closes it. If he was looking at this sensibly, Janice's departure should fill him with relief, but he can take no comfort. Silly bitch. Damned silly bitch. Sadness, sadness. Everything, then, was too late.

He locks the door, wanders into Herovit's office and goes to the scotch cache in the medicine cabinet above the basin. Conveniences of working in a maid's room—one could be self-sufficient. He takes out a fresh half-pint and examines it.

Well, this is against his policy, of course. It runs counter to everything he had planned to do. But what can he do now? There are excuses. Besides, what could a couple of belts this late in the day do to him? Herovit has conditioned the corpus to a high tolerance level for alcohol, the one useful bequest given him. Kirk lifts the bottle decisively and finishes off the half-pint as if he were drinking a can of beer.

Radiation, flushing, heat, palpitation as he flings the bottle into the wastebasket, but he has held it. All of the scotch is inside; Herovit's constitution is strong. "It isn't my fault," Kirk says to the typewriter, "and I'm not saying this because I'm drunk; the liquor hasn't even had a chance to hit me yet. No, that's the truth of the matter— I cannot be blamed for this one. I came into sequence too late, and writing is no damned preparation for life anyway. Let me tell you. What the hell could have been expected?"

The typewriter, a middle-aged IBM on which forty-three of the Survey novels have been typed, does not answer. It would not be equipped by its history to deal with questions this abstract. "Fuck yourself," Kirk says mindlessly and wanders off to the living room. He has the vague idea that he will now strip off his coat and in shirt-sleeves and ragged pants go striding manfully through all of Manhattan, showing the bastards on the pavements and in the streets that they cannot beat Kirk Poland—no sir, no one, nothing can beat Kirk Poland—but midway toward the door the idea arrests itself like a benign disease. He falls in place.

"This is ridiculous," he says and orders himself to at least get back to the couch if he is going to act like a damned fool (that traitor Herovit had had no capacity after all; why had he not remembered that?) but the order gets side-tracked and he rolls in place, babbling, frantic. He cannot move. He has been overcome. Was the scotch poisoned? So what if it was; what could he do now? Too much trou-

ble. Everything is too much trouble. He allows the scotch
to overtake him like a strait-jacket. Kirk sleeps.

20

Dreaming again. How many times has he dreamed, and
how has the quality of this shifted? Kirk does not know.
Now he dreams that he has indeed come to the science-
fiction conference at Lancastrian University, and after a
day of brief interviews with local press and disjointed out-
pourings to enormous audiences filled with people whose
language he does not know, he is now in a motel room,
making violent love to a coed whom he must have picked
up somewhere between the cocktail party and this moment.

The coed bears a ghostly similarity to Janice as she might
have been ten years ago, but her breasts are smaller and
unmarked; her thighs slide to easy accommodation, and he
finds that he does not have to think about Janice now. The
hell with her. "Oh, my God," the coed is saying—like all
of the adulteries she cannot, goddamnit, shut up—"You're
just the most wonderful writer I've ever read. You've been
a complete and basic influence on my life." He sucks on
her breasts while she continues tirelessly. "I used to read
you all the time when I was growing up; I would wait at
the newsstand for issues forecasting your new stories and
I went to back-date magazine stores to pick up the ones

I had missed. Alone! It was fabulous reading about the Survey Team, and I can't really believe that I'm in bed with Kirk Poland. I mean, it's like too much." He plays a genital glissando on her thigh and moves right in again; blinking, she offers him a breast.

"It's just the most incredible thing," she says, rubbing away at the back of his neck. "It's like this is happening to somebody else, not me, because I never thought I could have this kind of luck. Kirk Poland in bed with me. Incredible! That's right, do anything to me you want; I can't tell you how exciting all of this is. What I mean is that it's just a wonderful privilege."

Obviously this girl is really stupid. Despite the fact that she is a college student, she may even be a bit retarded, but what the hell, Kirk thinks, moving inside, anything can go to college these days, and besides, this is a fringe benefit. He should take it in that spirit. Normal people have pension plans and hospitalization coverage, comprehensive insurance and a rated family plan. He has found a stupid young girl who thinks that he is an important writer. *I am entitled to this,* Kirk dreams, rolling and rolling, yet cannot escape a feeling of pervasive guilt. If the girl is so consumately stupid, should he be taking advantage of her? Think of his better instincts. "Oh yes," she says as he comes into her for the fifth or sixth time that evening (in this dream he is a madman and there is no end to his resources), "yes, this is what I always wanted. Thank God I went to that party tonight, that I had the courage to walk up to you and say hello. I'm so grateful, so very grateful."

And so on and so forth. She will not keep quiet. Neither Herovit's women nor his, it would seem, understand the mysteries of silence. Kirk does what he can to draw the seed from himself, yanking it like threads tightening in his cells, and at last he is finished or in any event he quits (after five or six who can tell the difference?), lying then stunned and sated beside the girl. He knows that he will never think of sex again in his entire life. What a relief this will be!

"That was wonderful," he dreams she says, "absolutely fantastic. I knew that you'd be good because you're my favorite writer and we're soul-spirits together, but I didn't have the right to hope that you'd be *this* good." She is all right, he supposes. He is very glad they have met. Apparently his luck is changing at last.

"Why didn't you write me?" he says when he thinks it is time to talk, five minutes or hours later. "If you thought that I was so terrific you could have dropped me a line in care of the editors or like that. They forward that stuff." Sometimes.

"I wouldn't have thought of that. You were like a god to me; it was hard to believe that you would even pay attention."

"Really?"

"Oh, I don't feel that way any more," the girl says quickly. "Now I know that you're a person just like everyone, but not then. Oh, by the way," she says, springing with disconcerting haste from the bed, "by the way, I'd love to stay and reminisce with you some more, but I'm really afraid that I've got to be going now."

"What's that?"

"I mean, I have to get back to my apartment. I live with

my boyfriend, you see; most of us new-type college girls stay with our boyfriends. It's a very forward-looking place here, not like the old days, but my boyfriend is very hung up on roles, and he'll get pretty angry if I don't get back soon." Kirk grasps for her flesh, trying to retard her, but she seems, somehow, to have become amorphous.

"I know you'll understand," she says. "I had to come with you back to this motel because your desires are mine, but I can't get into any kind of long-term relationship. Science fiction is all very nice, but you outgrow it and go on to solid, meaningful long-term things, and this was really a goodbye to my youth."

"All right," Kirk says. He gives up and leans back on the bed as the girl dresses quickly, her back to him. The usual college-girl costume, he guesses: dungarees, sandals, a sweater (he has never been too strong on wardrobe details in his unconscious life).

"You know," he says, "you could have dropped me a line, I guess. Just to let me know that someone out there was reading the work. It wouldn't have taken much time; you could have made the effort." He notices the self-pity in this and stops, filled with disgust: self-pity was Herovit's problem, not his. (Even in dreams he thinks of Herovit.) Also, he does not like the edge of pain and regret which the girl seems to be vaulting him toward. It must be the implicit repudiation of her walking out on him; she does not mean enough to him otherwise.

"No, it wouldn't," she is saying. "It wouldn't have been right at all writing to you. There should be no personal contact between authors and readers because it gets you nowhere." Her voice has acquired an edge as well, a hard pierce, even a hysterical quality, of all things, and now she goes to the door of the motel room, flings it open and steps back, no longer looking at Kirk.

"All right," she says to someone outside the door. "I've done my part, I'm all finished. Now it's up to you," and yes, here they come, streaming through the door and advancing—all of them—upon the naked and quivering Kirk.

Here are the trustees of the university, heavy men with ponderous step and jowls; behind them are the division of academic affairs and the deans of men and women, no less, and behind *them* comes the full English faculty, wispy people wearing ceremonial robes and carrying medieval implements. Last of all is Wilk. He is wearing a business suit and seems rather embarrassed, as well he might be.

"I'm sorry about this," he says to Kirk, winking, twitching and shaking, "but it's all a research project, and as you know, I don't have any tenure. I don't even have a high school diploma, so I've got to cooperate with them pretty much down the line." As Kirk curls his legs fetally in the bed, trying for at least a little concealment, they press closer upon him in a small pack, the trustees at their head.

"You can't do this," the trustees are shouting, waving their fingers. "You have got to get control of your life; you cannot come here on a routine seduction and think that it is a solution because it is not, merely an evasion. This is not a science-fiction convention, you know." The English faculty brandish their implements; Kirk quivers and fixes his gaze on a series of cracks in the motel ceiling which might be an outline of the constellations.

"I'm sorry," he says, squeaking, "I'm sorry, I didn't know," thinking of the girl's treachery and what she has done to him, but the girl would have to be troubled herself to be involved in something like this. What a dream! "I can't stand this any more, damn it," Kirk says, but it is too late for such protestations, unconscious or otherwise ... for into the room now come the assembled research teams of the department of psychology, vigorous graduate assistants holding pads and pencils, shouting questions at him as the others back off to the walls and look on with satisfaction, some in hurried consultation with one another.

"How long did you fornicate with this girl?" the psychologists ask. "What did you think of it?" and "what precisely were your motivations, and what relationship would you say this bears to science fiction in the last third of the twentieth century? Is there any place for science fiction? Is there any place for the last third of the twentieth century? We demand to know this," the young psychologists, some of them quite demented, insist. "We have a right to our conclusions and our research; there are very few people who can help us as much as you can."

Oh yes, the universities seem to have changed a good deal since Kirk's unhappy two years upstate a long time ago. They are less formal and everyone seems quite enthusiastic, although this can hardly help him now. They are clustered too tightly for him to flee, and even in a dream he would not want to try elevation. "You bastard," he manages to whisper to Wilk during an eddy in the questioning. "How could you do this to me? How could you lure an old and trusted friend like this? Your stuff always stunk anyway. I've been meaning to tell you that for years," a routine professional insult which he regrets making.

"I told you," Wilk whispers. "I really had no choice in this. It was either cooperate or lose tenure; I can't really *write* anything any more, so I had to go along with this." A real son of a bitch, this Wilk, but no right to complain. Kirk should have thought of all of this before he accepted the invitation.

"Stop it!" he shouts finally, rearing from the bed, leaping for flight regardless before he remembers that he is still naked. The psychologists give a groan of delight and descend upon him then to examine his heartbeat with stethoscopes, his reflexes with hammers and watches, his gross skin temperature with small dangerous devices shaped like snails, his reaction time with needles. Like a cloud of aliens they settle upon him and begin to feed; he dreams that he tries to shrug free but his struggles are futile. They turn his strength against him and Kirk finds himself falling.

"All I wanted was a break," he shouts. "You have no right to do this to me, none of you," but he does not believe a word of this, he is getting what he deserved from the start . . . and so as the psychologists overtake him, the deans of men and women kneel to examine his tongue and eyes. The academic affairs committee moves off into a corner of the room to confer on a suitable statement for the press, and Wilk seems to disappear entirely, leaving Kirk on his own, the single representative of modern science fiction.

"Something is definitely wrong here," Kirk mumbles.

"This is not what I expected," and he awakens then stiff and strained on the couch, leaping and bounding on the pillows, the New York sun streaming greenly through his windows; the night is over. His first full day on this alien planet awaits. The strangeness of it. The grotesquery. It looks as bizarre as the dream but it is not as dark.

21

All right. Order this life. He must order it now. Call it dreamlike or real: Kirk finds himself charged with spirit as he springs from the couch. So much for somnolence if it will bring dreams like this; he will exist on the minimum of sleep until he has arrived at some point of balance. He goes prowling through the apartment, noting the litter of Herovit's life.

Empty drawers pulled out in Janice's section of the bureau, spots on the bathroom floor, little crumbs and blotches of milk spattered throughout the kitchen, floor, walls, refrigerator doors, small gifts to the household. The walls of the apartment wheeze out small, languorous odors through which he moves carelessly, opening the refrigerator, finding a glass of milk with coaster on top (a nauseating habit of Janice's). Milk has stayed there in this condition for weeks. The hell with it—he drinks it down quickly, finding it only slightly rancid, feeling it move within him to open

up channels of health and power. He belches enthusiastically, wringing out an a cappella progression of some in-
vention, and then goes into Herovit's office. Meet the
devil.

Here, the disorder is somewhat more complex. The
problems of the apartment outside this office are grubby
and domestic; they smack of old shoes, menstrual complaints and laziness. A determined housekeeper past
menopause would be able to clean up the outer apartment
in a matter of hours, but where would she begin, leaning
thick, fifty-year-old elbows on a broom, in this place?

On the desk is the typewriter. To the right and left of
the typewriter are cigarette scars, cigarette burns, sediment and stink from the fire, droppings of scotch, rubber
bands, paper clips, more paper clips, small wadded pieces
of paper, obscene doodles largely in the form of male
genitals or breasts carved in the desk top by a long-dis-
carded knife of his Middle Period, and so on, all of the
fragments with which the unfortunate Herovit had been
pacing out his days toward demolition. The end must have
been a relief. The carpet is pitted and frayed as well; on
its corners are manuscripts scattered in all stages of incom-
pletion, unanswered letters, collection notes of final judgment from various sources, and so on. The debris of three
years must lie on the floor of this office framing the work
area; perhaps Janice had been in three years ago to clean
it up, but then again she might not have been.

"Impossible," Kirk mumbles pointlessly. "This is impossible," but nevertheless there they are: carbons of the last
nine Survey novels; at least sixteen unsold short stories
which Herovit in disgust had chucked against the walls

after they had reached their last possible market (Mackenzie, that fine old man, refuses to market short stories—no percentage); several unmailed letters—some actually enveloped, addressed and stamped, others in intermediate stages of threat or desperation, all of them saved compulsively because Herovit could never tell when he might want to finish them or mail them or at least reread the lot to see what was on his mind twelve weeks ago. Many a blocked afternoon the unfortunate Herovit had spent scrabbling among his ruins, chuckling sadly over his unmailed rhetorical thrusts to the collection agents, magazine editors, lawyers and so on. Some of his best writing was definitely in these.

Also on the floor are science-fiction magazines and hundreds of loosely stacked paperbacks. The paperbacks are mailings from publishers to all members of the League for Science-Fiction Professionals which, unlike the guild, has a loose agreement with certain publishers to send new releases to the complete membership for their disavowal and regret. Others have been purchased by Herovit himself, out of pocket, to see what his enemies the competition were up to; they were always up to the same damned stuff, that was the answer.

Since it had been too much of an effort for Herovit, weakened by his sedentary life, to convey the paperbacks and magazines to the incinerator, and also too much of an effort for him to walk through them, the ridge of the carpet farthest from the desk in a westerly direction, that section under the window, had long since been established as a kind of neutral zone in which the paperbacks and magazines could nestle against one another unmolested. Perhaps they even copulated to produce more paperbacks and magazines because the growth was extreme—surely the publishers did not mail him *that* much.

"Sloppy," Kirk says. He feels a pure streak of puritanism arc and curve within him (color the streak pink or even crimson). "Sloppy, lazy, dirty, unkempt, disorganized," but then who is he to stand in judgment of the unfortunate Herovit, who had had such a difficult life? Run up against this ambivalence time and again, damn it; every time he thinks that he can take a position of clear determination and righteousness, counter-thoughts like these extrude. He will never get anything accomplished unless he takes a straight line of functioning and moves ahead without doubt, but he has misjudged the way things are here; there are always arguments on the other side. His early impressions of Herovit's life, formed largely by his lack of responsibility, are not standing up too well.

It was really quite complicated—nothing that could be cleaned up in a day or even in a week—and if Kirk was going to accomplish anything he was going to have to look at matters in terms of the long haul. One fast fuck with a prostitute or one conversation with Mackenzie was not going to do much. Of course Herovit had to be blamed for letting matters get to this state—Kirk wouldn't have let them get so out of hand—but then again, living Herovit's world from the inside was much worse than looking at it as a commentator; a dark, airless feeling sends bands across his chest which he hopes are not forerunners of a serious heart attack. Just tension. "Thanks so much for that," Herovit seems to murmur from a great distance or deep abscess. "I really appreciate this new understanding; it isn't quite so easy, is it?" "No," Kirk answers, "it is not that easy." "Well then, do the best you can; I'm going to take my rest," Herovit seems to say and then lies quiescent, a gnome in an anterior wall of the consciousness, quite relaxed, detached, bemused.

"Don't bail out on me now, you bastard," Kirk mutters, which is an unreasonable thing to say and unfair in the bargain (who put Herovit there that he should complain?), but Herovit laughs at him and snuggles deeper.

That would be the physical aspect of the office except for the walls. The walls, Kirk notes, are moist and dark, small cracks opening into the crevices of the building and emitting a complicated sort of fluid that might be the result of decay or independent growth. The closet behind the desk —not, properly speaking, part of the office at all—was another issue entirely. Kirk would not even know how to begin to deal with this one.

Inside the closet are copies of all the published novels— five or six or ten copies of each; in short, almost a thousand paperbacks of his own work—plus a couple of thousand magazines with his short stories, some of them dating back as far as 1955 and most of them never opened despite having been purchased in bulk lots at the newsstands at cover price. (Magazines never sent contributor's copies; it was another of the engaging traditions of the field.) Within the closet as well repose the Herovit files: carbons of all the letters that he did get around to mailing, replies to those letters, replies to the replies if necessary and so on—all of it stuffed clumsily into a row of small metal boxes picked up at junk stores (some with handles and some with none) and with absolutely no chronological order to the stuffing, so that letters dating from 1958 nestle in small balls against replies he wrote to other letters ten years later, and so on. Herovit had had his own kind of neatness, it would seem: what the bastard really was was a completist without a sense of order; the raw materials were there. What he needed was a full-time staff.

Also in the closet, lying in heaps on the crude shelves and eaves and floor are the carbons of all the original manuscripts of Kirk's published work, plus whatever originals the editors had seen fit to return to him after they had been through copyediting. He had had the idea that someday he would contribute these files to a university for an enormous tax deduction and even an honorary degree—a weird idea in the sixties—but when during the last few years the requests had started to come through from universities which, surprisingly, wanted this crap ... even then Herovit had not been able to cooperate, enormous tax deductions or not. (The honorary degrees had never been offered in the requests.) The closet by that time had become so disordered that it was impossible for the unfortunate Herovit to even open it without distinct feelings of horror; to actually get inside this wasteland for the task of collation would have been utterly devastating. He would never have gotten out of that closet. And so the manuscripts, like sick trees, had drooped and dropped their dead leaves from the shelves; they had showered them to the floor; they had fallen against one another and had become intermixed with dust and roaches . . . no, it was all impossible. Crazy.

You could simply not turn stuff like this over to the colleges even though the librarians writing the letters of solicitation had all said things like, "Rest assured we will receive your manuscripts in any condition you desire, since we have a staff anxious to compile, index and organize." But no graduate assistant, no matter how desperate and miserably in need of funds, would have been able to come to grips with this stuff. If he had (some thin youth with mad eyes bulging from their sockets, probing and poking through the Poland *oeuvre* in a cubicle on a dim high floor), the graduate would have made certain discoveries about the writer which the writer himself would not have been able to bear. No. No . . . Kirk takes a long look at the closed closet door and then turns away. It would be a fine thing to open it and throw all of this crap out, but he does not have the courage. One deep look inside that closet might unsettle him completely, and then where would he be? What would it all come to? What use would have been his life?

"Screw it," Kirk says. He rubs his hands on his thighs, then against one another, trying to force a certain briskness upon himself through this gesture. Busy, busy. Keep moving. What he should do, he supposes, is to go to the typewriter and do some writing. Real writing, writing of an elemental and vigorous nature which will free the bonds of his talent and start him at last on the worthwhile path he should have taken a decade ago . . . but he does not think that he is quite ready for writing. Not yet. Writing must come out of serenity, after all, and Kirk does not feel serene.

Furthermore, he will be unable to rely upon Mack or his Survey Team. It would have to be from the beginning, a new novel with new characters. A short story anyway. He does not even have the miserable fifty-one pages as a crutch to start off in new directions—not that he would miss them.

No, Kirk does not want to write. In fact, he never wanted to write, come to think of it. Who would want to be a writer? It was just a way of turning a fast buck at a bad time, and he had read enough of this garbage in his youth to be able to simulate it. There were any number of interesting things he could have done with his life; there was no reason not to break out of the trap at this time. A new man, a new life. Kirk enjoys the thought. Thirty-seven years old as he might be, he yet has options. Who ever *said* that he had to be a writer? Now, with Janice out of the house he does not have to pretend to be.

"I'm bailing out," Kirk says. He has gotten to talking aloud this morning; it is comforting and adds emphasis to his thoughts. "I'm quitting." Who would miss him? What audience? He has no audience. The only people who read him are in adolescent bedrooms or cross-country bus terminals. Goodbye to this. Kirk enjoys the thought. It is the best thing that has happened to him yet. The phone rings.

Not his office phone—that one has been ripped from the wall. This comes from the bedroom, and for just an instant he indulges the idiot thought that he will not answer. No calls, no connection. But he is as ritualistic as his predecessor. Easefully and then with growing anxiety as he cannot locate the phone (it is under bedclothes), Kirk goes to the bedroom and answers. Wilk? Mackenzie? Janice? No, it is Gloria from the Staten Island Association. Why not?

"I'm just down the block," she says shyly, her voice high and seemingly plaintive as it eases its way through him, "and I thought I might come up and say hello."

"What's that?"

"Unless you don't want me to come up. I'm sorry about that business on the phone the other day, but that's the way these things go."

"My wife left me yesterday." He could go on to say that it wasn't really *his* wife, just one by proxy, but it is too complicated. Forget it; he could never explain.

"Yes," she says softly, "I heard about that one. Word gets around."

"It does?"

"Well, yes. Science fiction is kind of a small, tight world, you know what I mean?"

"I noticed that."

"Anyway, I just happened to be in the neighborhood. It's nothing important; if you don't want me to come up—"

"I didn't think you were interested in science fiction," Kirk says, recalling something, "so how about that small tight world?"

"Well," she says with some nervousness—how shallow her self-confidence seems to be; all of these girls who Herovit has laid can be shattered so easily that it was impossible to know why he took them seriously—"I mean

if that's the kind of attitude you show, it isn't that important to me. I didn't know your personal situation; you
didn't even tell me you *had* a wife when you were at that,
uh, party. Of course I knew that but you thought you were
putting one over on me."

She sounds like the girl in the dream. Considered from
this aspect she does indeed. Maybe, Kirk thinks, this is
significant; maybe she was merely the trigger for that
dream. Regardless, why worry about it? Why look for motives, implications, levels of inference? This was Herovit's
bag. He was Kirk Poland, the man who would charge with
the times and let the situations flow where they would. So
what if she is the girl in the dream? The hell with this.
Flow. "Okay," Kirk says, "you want to come over, come
on. You know my address?"

"You bet."

"Then come on."

"Don't get certain ideas, Jonathan. I thought you could
use a friend, that's all, with your wife walking out on you.
But that's as far as it goes, you follow me? I wanted to be
kind."

"Right. Sure. It would be great to be kind. I couldn't put
it any better."

"Then look for me in a little while."

"Come over now," Kirk says, "don't wait, run. What the
heck, come right on over." He laughs what he hopes to be
a gay, free, uninflected laugh and puts down the receiver,
sitting with his hand on it for a time and then pulls the
sheets over the telephone and stands. At least that path
seems clear then.

Surely. He will have sex with this girl—her disclaimers he is sure are only to protect her ego—which will at least keep his mind off more urgent problems, and from then on he will work out some interesting way to spend the remainder of his life. Sex will not be an escape, but then again, the Glorias of this world must find their uses somehow and this would be one of them. What else could she be good for? What else was Janice ever good for? She had found her true role as a somewhat seductive member of the Honor John Steele Society and had never reached that point of utility again. For Janice everything had had to go wrong at twenty-three or so; it was her ill luck to have found a position which she would have to outgrow. Herovit had had the same problem in a more complex way.

Clean the apartment. Like the dining room. What will this girl think of him, otherwise? The trouble is that he cannot begin to clean in the time he has, and as he thinks this over, he decides not to apologize. The filth will inform her with pity for him. She will want to clean it up herself, blaming the trouble on Janice. He will not bother. Leave it lay. There are intricacies to almost anything. He sees Mack Miller.

"Excuse me," Mack says, appearing in a corner of the dining room, as corporeal and stolid as ever, wearing full space gear. Only his eyes are visible through the gray helmet, staring blankly through the visor, sweeping Kirk and the walls as if seeking a dangerous alien. His hand carries a flat object that must be a weapon. "I want to talk to you, because this really can't keep going on, you know."

"Forget it," Kirk says, trying to hold on to his composure. "Where did you come from anyway? I dealt with you last night."

"That's quite impossible," Mack says. His gear clanks as he places himself against the wall, not moving toward Kirk but not really opening up any distance either. "You've been living with this for thirteen years, and your little neurotic outbursts don't have anything to do with it, I'm afraid. You can't sever a relationship with dreams, and I want to try and bring you to your senses before it's too late."

"I haven't been living with you," Kirk says patiently. "It's the other guy. Herovit. As far as I know, I have no relationship with you at all."

"That's what I'm saying. You're going to make a terrible mistake. Can't you see that? For all I know it's probably too late already. You're being warned, Herovit; you'd better get hold of yourself."

"The name isn't Herovit. It's Kirk. Kirk Poland."

Mack lets out a grim laugh, bending slightly and adjusting various metal clips at knee-level. He must be using the amplificator; his voice is high-pitched and unnatural; Kirk does not recall Mack as having sounded this way before, but then Mack is in full gear, the dress uniform of the Survey Team, obviously scouting out new terrain. "Please stop this nonsense," Mack says, "because we simply don't have the time for it. If you want to change your life you're going to have to risk some real changes, and I don't mean this disassociative garbage. You'll have to utilize full scouting procedure." He inclines his helmet. "Don't you understand that?"

"Get out of here."

"You don't want me out."

"Yes, I do."

"I'm on a mission," Mack says, running gloved fingers over the wall, filtering out pieces of plaster. "And we never quit a mission in Survey."

"Please."

"You can't get rid of me," Mack says with conviction, snapping at his viewplate. "I wouldn't be here if you didn't really want me. Don't you know that? Don't you see what's going on by this time, alien Herovit?"

"The name is Poland."

"Time's running out, Herovit. How much longer did you think you could go on this way? You've been pushing your luck for a long time on this planet; now you're past the limit. We've had you under observation for a long time, and now we're going to make our move." Mack shows him the flat thing in his hand. "See? I hope I don't have to take these extreme measures but if they prove necessary—"

"Get out of here," Kirk says shakily. "I'll kill you if you don't."

"Hah!" Mack says and turns a button on the amplificator so that his voice booms louder. "You'll what?"

"Forget it," Kirk says. "Forget that part altogether."

"Sad," Mack says, running his hands over his space gear. "Sad, sad. Don't you think it's time you faced up to this?"

"You're dealing with the wrong man."

"Look, Herovit, here in Survey we have no taste for discussion. Activity, violent accomplishment is all we

understand," Mack says, and indeed he does seem a little
out of place in Kirk's dining room, the clumsy space garb
making an unusual picture against the clutter of unwashed
dishes, Natalie's empty crib and so on. Mack looks medita-
tively again at the thing in his hand. "I think—" he says.

"Please," Kirk says, raising his hands. He finds that he is
terrified. Undignified, perhaps, but he has never seen
Mack this close up; the aspects of menace are clear, and
beyond that there was something about Mack he had
missed—how could he have missed it? It is a factor of
subtle *cruelty* . . .

"I'm sorry about that business," he says this morning. "I
must have been drunk and anyway—"

Mack makes a dismissive gesture. "Means nothing," he
says. "You don't think your pitiful efforts at Survey sabo-
tage have any effect upon me, do you?"

"No. Of course not. Never."

"I'm going to be reasonable," Mack says, tugging on his
visor and putting the weapon away. "See, I am not without
mercy. I'm going to leave you to think all of this over at
leisure, and then I'll come back and we'll finish up."

"Go," Kirk says weakly. "Good. Fine. Just leave, then."

"For a little while—so you can ponder the risks, Herovit.
You see," Mack says quietly, beginning to waver, "you've
looked at this wrong, Jonathan; see, I'm taking the time to
talk to you. You didn't get rid of me, you lost something
you imagined to be me, a thought projection cunningly
placed in your mind by the Team to displace the issue, but
not for a moment was it me. Time is running too short,
however, as I said, and you're going to have to come to

some basic re-alteration of your thought processes quite rapidly. You'll see me shortly and we'll work everything out."

"You talk very well," Kirk says. "I never thought somehow you'd sound this good."

"Well," Mack says with a little modest laugh, "part of our training, of course, is to adjust to local conditions. Please don't stare at me that way, Jonathan, it's no good for your eyesight." Mack rises slowly against the wall, puffing out small jets of steam from the evacuator capsule on the back of his space gear, then vaults to the ceiling. He becomes translucent and dissolves, a tricky device of matter transference in which the Team has been well-schooled. First Mack's limbs vanish, then his torso (for a moment, Kirk thinks that he can see Mack's internal organs; the matter-transference device is not smoothly integrated it would seem), and the last thing to go is Mack's head—the contents of the helmet, that is—for the helmet itself remains for quite a time, revolving slowly against the ceiling, looking from this angle like a small planet (or maybe Kirk means asteroid—his astronomy has never been that hot).

"You son of a bitch," he says to the ceiling after Mack is gone. "You can't do this to me." Not that this does him any good; the aliens may curse in their strange tongues after Survey has paid a visit, but not a single alien has ever been spared Mack's retribution once the peace was made. Nevertheless he says again, "You can't do this to me," banging open the kitchen door in frustration and leaving the accursed room.

No sense to it; this is really preposterous. Here he wanted to make it Kirk's world, and progressively it looks like Herovit's. The pointlessness of it all. It is enough to make him despair. Nothing has worked out. Nothing is going right. The buzzer sounds as it would have to eventually—he cannot avoid this—and someone who distortedly sounds like Gloria babbles through the intercom.

22

Wilk is along.

He follows her cautiously, and as he and his old, old friend exchange stares, matters begin for the first time to fall together meaningfully for Kirk. Not in the easy, mechanical way that they did with the prostitute, but on a more subterranean level. The world begins to make sense to him in its weary, banal way; there are only so many confrontations possible or so many sequences of events; given its chance, the tired world, like a hack writer, will settle at the easiest level of accommodation. Not for the sake of structure, but because it has nothing else on its mind, no better idea.

Anyway, as all of them have been saying for quite a time, science fiction is indeed a small, tight world. Only five or six hundred people in the country write it with any success at all; only another few thousand are involved to the point of being constant readers; and if you are going to meet up with someone you probably will, if not tomorrow, then by the week after next at the latest. Also, there is a delimitation in the field; for all of the manifest possibilities which its writers and editors always discuss at conventions, the truly great things to be done, events and plots revolve in the same weary combinations in their own lives. They marry one another's spouses, carry on feuds for forty years, and so on. This is really, despite the reputation it has gotten in the newsmagazines, a very cautious, conservative little area, this science fiction. It is like an association of undertakers or dog handlers. Locales change, but the events and people are the same.

Wilk seems more subdued than previously. His stare holds, then flickers off to that spot on the wall where Mack had last been seen, then comes back and flicks off again as he puts a long, palpitating hand on his goatee. This, however, may be more an outcome of having been in bed with Gloria of the Staten Island Association for many hours; Kirk's memory on the point cannot be trusted, but he thinks that she was quite an energetic fuck, grinding out spirit and semen alike with dispatch. Then again Wilk may only be adopting a funereal judiciousness. "Terribly sorry about your situation," he says, letting go of his beard with some reluctance and extending a hand which Kirk does not touch. "A bad thing altogether, but then she was never the right person for you anyway, Jonathan. Her track record is a very bad one; even in the old *Wonder* Reader days, you know, a lot of problems. Many problems there; here was a girl who was frigid before she was deflowered. Still there's no accounting for the things that happen to us, eh, my friend?" Wilk says, peering with rather insane eyes (why had Herovit never noticed this? why, of course, that was it, Wilk was mad) into the open office looking for, Kirk supposes, a fresh bottle of scotch. Wilk will never know the secret of the cache.

"You didn't say you were with someone," he points out to Gloria. It seems the most reasonable line of conversation; he could try explaining to Wilk that he is not Herovit but someone else, but this would be far too complex . . . and furthermore, he does not believe it. He is not sure who he is; in other circles this would be called an identity problem. What are they doing here? "It would have been nice, you know, if you had at least told me."

She shrugs, a fine-looking girl for all the faint facial puffiness that in no more than ten years will be indolence and spite, for all the misshapen aspect of her breasts, which unlike Janice's do not look at all well in clothing. "Well," she says, "it didn't seem so necessary. Anyway, what did you think I had in mind for coming up here? Don't get any peculiar interpretations now."

"I didn't think. I never think."

"Well, that's good. Keep on not thinking."

"Too bad about Janice," Wilk burbles, "although my sympathies must be qualified. Do you think, by the way that I might be able to bother you for a short one? Just a touch. It's pretty well on in the day and I find New York hard to take. You're anesthetized to it, obviously, but I don't think that I could ever take it again. It's been years since I was in the city this long; you get a trapped feeling very quickly."

"You were the girl in his hotel room the night before

last," Kirk says. "I spoke to you and you knew who it was and you wouldn't tell me."

"The scotch, Jonathan," Wilk says. "I was talking about some scotch, remember?" *Leave me out of this,* his rather tormented eyes seem to be saying. Wilk too has touched limits. Whether this can be ascribed to New York, who knows?

"What girl are you talking about?" Gloria says. "I don't think you know what you're saying."

Fury now curls from the edges of Wilk's goatee and emerges in a small, wormlike smirk which crosses his features quickly and then is gone, leaving a trail. "I wouldn't try to overanalyze situations," he says in a high-pitched voice. "It just leads to all sorts of complicated troubles and doesn't get us anywhere. This is a condolence call. Didn't I ask you for a scotch? It seems to me I'm sure I did."

"He seems to think that I was in your room the night before last."

"Nothing," Wilk says uncomfortably. "It means nothing, these suspicions." He seems to give up on the concept of scotch, walks to the office window instead, putting a shoulder through an intricate, almost geometrical series of gestures which may show fey dismissal but then again might reveal brain damage. Hard to tell with science-fiction writers; it could be both. "Jonathan is always talking. He talks a great deal and always did from the time I knew him. A genuinely speculative mind. It seems to me that this condolence visit is not going in the proper direction. Jonathan, I've asked you several times for a drink, and although this lack of hospitality could be put down to bereavement or nervous shock, I think that it's beginning to get ridiculous now."

"I heard you perfectly well. You've asked me for a scotch. But if the truth must be told, I don't care to give you one, and I think that you should get off that stuff."

"Just like you, eh? Following a noble example. Well, indeed," Wilk says, turning from the window now with the air of a Man Restored—all doubts seem to have been put away along with the hope for scotch—"I can see that we're well into pointlessness. You can't accept the fact that we stopped by as friends because we thought you could use some intelligent company to take your mind off your, uh, new marital situation, but if you're going to become vindictive, there's no reason for us to be here. None at all. You really only have yourself to blame for this; it's not my decision that your wife stepped out on you. Gloria, let's leave this man," Wilk says absently, reaching out a hand to grasp her palm and tug. "This is getting us nowhere."

"I still want to know why she was in your hotel room." Mack Miller would not have to put up with this shit. Mack Miller, in fact, seems to be observing all of this from a near remove and looking upon it with increasing rage, the fluorescence of space dancing and dazzling off his garbs as with arms folded, he makes an evaluation. Mack knows exactly what should be done with people like this, and yes, Kirk agrees, he is right.

"That is beside the point," Wilk says. "I think that our business here is being concluded."

"You see," Kirk says with a desperate reasonableness—attend, Mack, and see how he is trying to lever the situation with calm—"I don't really mind what you do—the way you live your life is of very little interest to me—but I don't want to feel faceless, and when I know that you were with this bastard, who not so incidentally represents everything against which I've fought—"

"Oh, come on," Wilk says. "It's one thing to deny a man a drink but entirely another to start with this nonsense. Gloria, let's go. I can see that the man is torn beyond reason by grief, and we have better things to do than to argue in this way—"

"I think I'll stay a while," Gloria says, giving a maternal wink which may be addressed toward Kirk, but then again, may take in Natalie's crib. "This is very interesting. I want to hear more of this."

"I demand that you go," Wilk says excitedly. Agitation causes his goatee to shift across his features, moving up and down in a rapid motion like an unusual kind of pendulum. "There's no basis for this. We come for one reason and this man gives us another. This is an order."

"I don't want to be ordered. Besides, you have no control over my life. You think you may, but you don't. I'll stay until I'm ready to go."

"Damn it," Wilk says, "this is my expense account you're living with." He gives Kirk a pleading look. "I don't suppose you'd be more reasonable if I suggested we go downstairs and have a quiet drink together, the two of us outside, would you?"

"He wouldn't be any more reasonable than you are," Gloria says. "In fact you're both the same, you're exactly the same kind of person. How can you ask him to be reasonable?"

"Please," Kirk says. He feels out of his depth now, the same way he used to during Janice's intense and severe dialogues with the baby, her whispered conversations with anonymous people over the telephone in which he knew that she was murmuring the most terrible indecencies about his life and health habits, yet he could not find the strength to go in and listen on an extension. "Couldn't you take your personal difficulties somewhere else, like outside? I'm afraid that I've got a great deal on my mind now and I really can't get into the middle of this. I can't even bear to listen to it, as a matter of fact. If you have something to settle between you, I'd very much like to be left out of this, I really would."

"Oh, I really don't care myself," Wilk says with a gesture of disgust. "It doesn't matter to me one way or the other. I'm withdrawing the invitation, by the way. I think that your conduct has been atrocious, and you're quite beyond my abilities to redeem you. You're just one of those people who should have gotten out of the field years before, Jonathan, because you can't stand up to it at all."

"You want to bet I can't stand up to it? You don't know who you're talking to, that's your trouble."

"Look," Wilk says, gesturing toward the girl who—arms folded, nostrils distended—is looking at all of this with dispassion, "just take her, all right? Take her off my hands. I thought it would be a friendly thing to drop by this morning, it was completely my idea; I thought we could help you pick up the pieces by taking your mind off it, but if this is all I'm going to see, the hell with it. You're completely unqualified. You *have* the girl; go on, take her. I'm finished."

"Don't you walk out on *me,*" Gloria says. "You've got a lot of gall if you think that an aging bum like you can walk out on *me.* I'm going to walk out on *you.*"

Kirk sees what will happen next. Fated, it is. They will desert simultaneously, racing each other to the door, hands grasping for the knob, feet in full sprint, the winner to be the one first out the door, receiving the emblem of desertion. The other will be the abandoned. Meanwhile, as they do this, the floors will shake; his own body, made rather questionable by strange physical activities and abuse, will shudder. *Now you're thinking along the right lines, friend,* he hears Mack Miller say. It seems that it has always been this way: whether Herovit, or now Kirk, he has always been there as a witness while around him people work out their miserable emotional situations and use him as focus. There might even be a medical name for this —a terminology, so to speak. *Herovit's Syndrome,* they would call it. A subvariety of neurasthenia worthy of special annotation in the literature. *Herovit's Syndrome* could stand exploration; he might be able to lease himself out to the American Psychiatric Association. *You're getting on the beam,* Mack says, getting ever closer; that's the way it should have been. *Think of yourself, not the aliens.*

"Okay," Kirk says, striding to the door. "I'm going to resolve this simply because I'm the one who's going to leave. You can settle this thing nicely between yourselves or even move into the apartment together. Sublet it; I

can't pay the rent anyway. I'll find new quarters, and
when I'm settled, you can arrange to ship me the pieces
you don't like. Wouldn't that be the fair thing to do?"

They stop in mid-stride (Gloria in the lead by a neck)
and look at him with some astonishment. People enmeshed in *Herovit's Syndrome,* the APA will notice, do
not appreciate having their rituals broken. "What is this?"
Gloria says. "Are you completely insane? This is your life;
don't you believe in it?"

"Not any more," Kirk says, and he knows that this is the
truth, not a Mack Miller nodal implantation in his occipital
area. "Not really at all."

"I've canceled your invitation. We cannot tolerate this
at Lancastrian."

"You told me that, Mitch. I heard you already. I don't
want to go."

"You don't know what you're missing."

"Oh, I think so," Kirk says, thinking of his dream. "I
think I do. Anyway, I want to count on that, Mitch, because you see I'm quitting science fiction anyway, so as you
can see it would be a waste of money and the time of the
university to appear under false pretenses. They'd be talking to an ex-science-fiction writer and that would affect
your own position. I'm walking out of this apartment. I'm
leaving my life. Look here, I really mean it, I'm not just
saying this."

He charges to a closet, seizes his overcoat while noting
with a curse that Janice has managed to somehow take his
small private suitcase that had been there for years in the
event he had to make a quick and final exit. There were

even fifty dollars there in a secret compartment. Well, at least he wants to take his toothbrush. He goes off to the bathroom to look for it. Kirk is not sure when he last brushed his teeth—five or six years ago anyway; nonetheless, a horrid sense of neatness has been invoked which the Survey Team, anyway, would understand. It would be improper to start on a new life without a toothbrush. You never knew when you might want to exercise good dental hygiene: it could be in Times Square while checking out the all-night movie theatres; it might be before entering the quarters of another prostitute or looking up an employment agent. It is best to be prepared regardless. The urge to create oral antisepsis could strike anytime. At thirty-seven his teeth, after long abuse, might be ready to fall out of his mouth. Precautions: take precautions.

Also, as long as he is in the bathroom, he might as well take the unopened box of prophylactics—Rameses, they are—from the medicine chest. These were the ones that he had purchased hopefully soon after Janice gave birth, just to have on hand . . . until he found that she believed herself to be allergic to them or at least terrified that a Rams might fall off him in extremis to become permanently lodged within. Whatever it was, he had never used them. He has, as a matter of fact, never used any kind of prophylactic device in his life except for masturbation (which is a different thing altogether and hardly to be discussed). After so many years of casually fornicating without consequence, he and Janice had simply believed themselves to be infertile. Or blessed. Stupid fools.

Ah well, live and learn. He returns to Wilk and Gloria,

who do not seem to have moved. Has he really had such a stunning effect upon them? *Good boy,* Mack says, so near that he does not even have to use the amplificator. *You're very close now. Just another step and you'll be where we want you to be. One more. It's so easy.* Probably not; he will never overestimate himself again. He stuffs the various items into his inner jacket pockets, dons his overcoat. "The rent is due on the first of the month, of course," Kirk says, "but the landlord is a pretty big corporation, and I don't think he'd mind if you sent it a little bit late. You can divide it up anyway you want or sublet it when Mitch goes back to school or whatever you say. Usually I paid around the fifteenth or twentieth of the month and no one ever complained. Anyway, all of this has something to do with urban renewal; I think that he's trying to sell the building anyway. For relocation. Anything else I have to tell you? No, I think that's pretty thorough; if you have any questions you can drop me a line care of General Delivery. Manhattan. I ought to be around for a while to pick up the mail, anyway." He is rambling. All right, so be damned. He is entitled to musings, jottings, stream of consciousness. Isn't he, Mack? *Stop thinking,* Mack says, *actify.*

"This is ridiculous," Gloria says. "This is really ridiculous. I don't know what I'm in the middle of, but will you both stop it, please?" Her voice, however, does not carry the message, not quite at all; it comes from being overwhelmed rather than moving above the situation, and from experience Mack can detect that the self-assurance has been worked out. All of it, all of it was easy. He should have moved in and handled it from the outset, rather than letting the others let it go this far. He looks at the alien nostrils, the alien features of these people in his room, and feels a pure, mean surge of competence arc through him: it was another job for Survey, was all.

"Stop it," the female alien is still saying. "Just leave me alone. I don't know why I ever got involved with people like you. You've all got to be crazy. Crazy."

"You don't have to react this way," the male alien says, moving alertly to block Mack's path into the hallway. "I mean I realize it's very disturbing, what's happened to you recently and losing a wife, but then again it could work out very nicely. Look at how I've done. When my second wife walked out on me I was just shattered. You know how I felt about Anna, don't you? Preposterous girl, but I thought it would never be the same again, but it all worked out wonderfully. And then when Muriel and I broke up years after that, I had that feeling again, but it was just panic— pure panic—and you'll find that you'll adapt wonderfully well. Life is a matter of changes, stages," the male alien adds, casting its features in an attempt at shrewdness in the manner of their strange planet, and by this time Mack knows exactly how to handle them. He moves out the door, turning and driving a metaled fist deeply into the face of the male. It shrieks, the female behind it makes fluttering gestures, and Mack laughs with the power of it and then darts toward the steps.

"Watch it," Mack says, "just watch it. You're being spared for the moment, but this is only a temporary policy, we'll be back later." Then he is gone, scooting down the stairwell onto the alien terrain, freed of the aliens at last, trembling within his spacesuit but eased, eased and confident. He finds his way out of the building, in which he has never been before, through his marvelous access to the telepathicator, which gives him access to the memories of the corpus which he has tenanted. He comes to the new ground of the strange world and looks around him, his hands tight and ready, grasping the holsters below his belt.

But then, looking at the bodies of the aliens strewn before him, Mack knew that now, it could have been no other way. The liberals and would-be progressives could whine, Headquarters could raise questions, the members of the Survey themselves could doubt . . . but Mack knew that it was this way and would be no other, so long as the Team was there to do the jobs that no one ever would.

There was always, at any time of history, a group of men who would get the job done. They would have to do it outside of the rules, they would have to do it counter to the approved tactics of the ruling branches or hierarchies, but in the last analysis it was they upon whom the fate of humanity depended because they could get the job done however nastily and accept the nastiness. That was the meaning of a Surveyman. It would always be this way. Murder would have to be part of it from time to time and other things as well and at every step Headquarters would resist and the bleeding hearts would yelp but now, still the job would be done.

That was the meaning of a Surveyman.

That was Mack's duty as the inheritor of the Team.

Kicking aside the dead alien with a grunt, Mack went on his way.

Kirk Poland: Survey Sunlight

23

At the first alien intersection, Mack attacks and knocks unconscious with a blow a male alien; sprinting down the peculiar walkways of the planet, he manages to inflict injury upon several others. But by weight of numbers the pursuers, calling for aid from the alien reinforcements, wear him down, and at last Mack finds himself trapped in a pathway as they descend upon him. He feels his power rushing from him, the force of his rage now the only defense, and realizes with horror that he is too old for this. He should have been retired some time ago; he can no longer meet the physical requirements of Survey. Nevertheless, he will fight onward, perish with his armor on, crying defiance to the aliens who spring upon him and make him give up progressively more of his position. Something must save him. It always has before. And if it does not he has the assurance that he has done his work well.

He moves to an open space. An alien vehicle hits him with terrific force, striking through his armor, and he falls helpless to the hard, gray earth, flailing. He feels the pain become part of him, and yet it is not a part of him; it is outside, deflecting his rage inward, and as he lies rooted in place Mack babbles with the fury of his knowledge, trying to stand. He cannot. He feels his vital juices ooze from him, a Surveyman's last testament, as the gabbling aliens move in closer around. "Kill," he mutters to himself. "Kill, kill, kill, kill, kill," and orders his body to rise for one last striving, but the noble body, reliable for so long, will not obey, the strong, once-competent hands curl in anguish over the stones, and it moves beyond a question of will. "Kill," he says to himself in the old way, trying to find some resource and function, but there is nothing.

Only then does his control go. He has held out for so long; surely he is entitled. He finds himself sobbing in a manly way, begging himself to rise, yet weeping because he cannot. "It isn't fair," Mack says, shaking his head, rotating over the stones, now conscious that his limbs have abandoned him. "This shouldn't be, something is terribly wrong, it shouldn't have been this way, the dirty sons of bitches," and then says no more. The gallant old heart has given out in his Surveyman's prime. He feels warmth, enclosure, encrustation, erosion and ascension—a microcosm of a Surveyman's fate—and then Mack is risen again, triumphant and reborn, howling out his defiance over a thousand tenements as the alien sun rises and the alien sun sets and all of it begins again, but in some other place or time.

ABOUT THE AUTHOR

Barry N. Malzberg was born in New York City and received an A.B. degree from Syracuse University, where he was subsequently a Shubert Playwriting Fellow. He has published a number of novels, and his work has appeared in most of the major magazines and anthologies in the field of science fiction. He lives in New Jersey with his wife and two children.